Red Door

A L A N   M c G I L L

Red Door

CONTENTS

Blood is red
Bruises are blue
We hid behind the Red Door
And so should you!

PROLOGUE

Castle Parlimae rested on the edge of a giant mountain, just across a big ravine. It overlooked and protected the village of Parlimae, a place inhabited by artisans, craftsmen, farmers, and the many families who had served the Parlimaes for generations.

The fields behind the village supplied the grains that fed the land. Livestock were plentiful and enjoyed grazing in the lush fields that lay between the village and the Dark Forest. The vast expanse of mighty trees was so thick in places that not even the daylight kissed the ground.

The Dark Forest was a place to be feared. Murderers and thieves made homes in hidden villages. Only the foolish or truly desperate traveled through without an armed escort. But there was something else that lurked in this dangerous place. An evil whose thirst was never quenched.

Lord Parlimae was a good steward of his lands. He kept his people safe from the hideous creatures rumored to lurk in the woods. Everyone always had plenty to eat and a roof over their heads. Life was good . . . until it was not.

Lord Parlimae's wife died giving birth to his only son, William. The boy had all a young noble could want. His father indulged his every desire and would do anything to protect his only living heir. But Lord Parlimae could not protect his son from his own heart.

William was the eldest child in the land for many years. His only friends were a peasant girl named Alessandra and a farm boy named Seth. For years, the three of them were inseparable, enjoying a bond as one often does with childhood friends. As William entered manhood, he developed feelings for Alessandra that went beyond friendship. Unfortunately, she did not share his affections.

Years later, Alessandra would be forced to leave the village of Parlimae and forgo her true name. She'd become the Duchess of Harcourt and, eventually, my friend. But this is not that story. It is the love story between mi Lady Alessandra and Seth. It is also the story of the emergence of the black wolf, a hideous werewolf who terrorizes the village, the Dark Forest, and my friend.

Three friends. Two will fall in love. One will go mad.

Much like Father Daniel at the Abbey of Feldberg, who keeps a chronicle of night creatures and other strange facts, I have decided to tell this story so we may know the truth about mi Lady and Seth. This is a love story. It is their story.

May the Lord bless and keep you,

Francis Altier

Humble servant and carriage driver to the Duchess of Harcourt

Seth and Alessandra

ONE

NOBODY LOOKS
FOR THE LIVING
AMONG THE DEAD

usic carries on cold nights when all is quiet, people are asleep, and not much else is stirring. Under the light of the moon, the buildings on either side of the main street cast long shadows. The village is empty and void, dark yet bright.

A beautiful woman in a long, white dress slowly walks down the center of town. A thin strap of her dress falls from her shoulder. She carries a violin in one hand, the bow in the other. Her curly blonde hair sways gently as she moves.

On a night when you can see your breath, she should be freezing with bare feet. She passes a few houses. Candles sit in the windows. They flicker in the dark, but the homes are black within.

All around the tiny village, tall trees hide the landscape from the moon's light. They're like black curtains, covering and comforting yet mysterious.

She places the violin under her chin. We can almost see her face, but not quite. She begins to play, slowly drawing the bow across the strings. The sound is haunting and melodic. Her thin fingers press the neck of the instrument to produce music as beautiful as she. The notes drift through the air, ribbons of sound led by a treble clef that fan out across the village and move through the darkened alleys, beyond the shadows, and above the high trees that surround the small town.

The soles of her feet move quietly across the ground. Her toes sink into the mud. The moon's rays glisten over her skin. Her dress leaves little to the imagination.

She moves effortlessly, the haunting sounds matching her steps. The music grows louder and louder, summoning candles to the windows of nearby houses. Their flames flicker, matching the speed of her play.

As she passes an alley, the home to her right shows movement. A man stands in the window, the candle on the sill providing just enough light to see a small portion of his face. He is mesmerized by the sound, staring blankly through the glass.

The moon's rays reveal the expressionless faces of a husband and wife in the house across the street. They stand at the window in their nightgowns, hypnotized by the violin and watching the street.

After the violinist passes, those who had come to the windows fade from sight. The candles go out abruptly, and the houses go dark. When she approaches a new set of homes, the inhabitants emerge to witness her performance, then disappear once she has moved on.

Just ahead, the hillside at the end of town is black. Yellow eyes flicker in the night. As she plays, a howl grows from the darkness. It rises to meet her music, matching the intensity. The melody runs through her body, causing a shiver of fear and excitement.

The woman continues to walk forward with the violin tucked under her chin. Her steps slow, but her song remains the same. The wolf's howl slows, too, following the pace of her instrument. She moves from one side of the street to the other, crossing through the village as if the sound flows from her soul.

The music is so powerful that it summons nature. Gray vines sprout from the ground, climbing up the sides of buildings and homes. Some wrap themselves around porch posts. Entire houses lose themselves to the sinister foliage.

Red thorns sprout on the vines, sharp and deadly with a poison that seeps from their points like drops of blood. As the music continues, droplets fall, striking the ground. Each hit produces a slight sizzle. The liquid is so deadly that it damages everything it comes in contact with, even the dirt.

Her song directs the movement of the vines. They stop growing, giving way to red-and-black buds that erupt into beautiful flowers. A sweet aroma fills the air as the petals open, the soothing smell complementing the melodic tones she continues to play.

A hand reaches out slowly from behind the violinist, trying to grasp her shoulder. Seemingly unaware, she continues to draw her bow across the violin. The moon's light illuminates her, follows her.

She moves just beyond the hand's reach, never breaking stride or changing the song. She doesn't react to the threat at her back but takes a few steps forward in her march through town. The hand rises again— another attempt to touch the violinist—but she's just out of reach.

She zigs down the street. A moment later, she zags to the other side, following the tempo of the music. The hand tries to grab her once more. This time, it reaches its target.

The need to see her, to understand her, is almost palpable. Who is this mysterious woman? Why is she playing this strange and haunting song in the middle of the night?

As the hand begins to turn her, a woman's scream tears through the night. Eyes come into focus. Daylight replaces the night. A man's voice gets louder and louder until it is nearly a shout.

"Ally! Ally! Wake up," Seth said, shaking her lightly. She had drifted off to sleep but awakened as she screamed out. She leapt at him, wrapping her arms around his neck, her chest heaving as she tried to catch her breath. He held her tight. "It was just a dream. It's OK. It's OK, you're safe."

She looked around, a bit confused.

"That must have been some nightmare," he said, pulling back to brush the hair out of her face. "You were talking in your sleep."

"What was I saying?" Alessandra asked as her breathing began to return to normal.

"Nothing really. You just repeated 'no' a couple of times and something about a woman. You said 'why' a few times too. Then you jolted up with a scream," he said. "What was it about?"

"I don't know. I don't remember much," she said, standing. Now that she was fully awake, she realized it was just a nightmare. As she buttoned her blouse, she took a few steps toward the gate. Seth finished pulling on his boots, then fastened his shirt as he walked up behind her. He slowly wrapped his arms around her from behind. "You OK?"

She leaned back, resting her head against his chest. With a smile, she turned around and kissed his lips softly. "I'm always OK when I'm with you."

Alessandra looked out across the cemetery toward the church. The old, abandoned building and this graveyard were all that was left of a once-forgotten village deep in the forest.

"You ever wonder what happened here?" she asked, walking toward the cemetery gate. They were careful not to touch the red-and-black flowers that covered it. Even though she and Seth didn't know the history of this place, they could tell there was something strange about the plants from the first time they visited.

The flowers were pretty—mostly black with red accents—and the sweet smell was intoxicating. But that was the deception. The gray vines that held the beautiful flowers also sprouted sharp, red thorns that seeped a poison. Bloodred droplets dripped to the ground, leaving behind small, acidic circles where the droplets burned the dirt as well as any grasses or plants it came into contact with.

"Remember when we first came here?" she asked, looking at the thorns.

"Yes. Of course. Two dead highwaymen. A thorn stuck in the hand of one. I remember it well. You made me bury them."

"And the other dead guy was torn up. Mauled by something," she added.

"Probably a wolf. We did see some right after we found the bodies. And there had been reports of wolves running through the forest. Killing livestock and some even threatening villagers," Seth said.

As she looked at the flowers covering the gate, she remembered that fateful day. Both she and Seth had grown up in the village of Parlimae and played for years in these lands. They knew the forest well, but they never came this far from the castle, so neither of them had ever heard of this place before. Not even William, their childhood friend, knew of its existence. And he knew the land better than anyone.

His father owned most of this area of the country. As the son of the nobleman from Castle Parlimae, William was set to inherit everything someday. His father, Lord Parlimae, treated Alessandra like a daughter. She, William, and Seth were roughly the same age, so they spent their youth together.

But nobody had ever spoken of an old, secret village in the forest. The town of Mercel was the only hidden village anyone ever talked about, and it was a few hours' ride west on the well-traveled forest road.

Something about her dream seemed familiar, and not just the vines and flowers spirited on by the music. This made her quiet and pensive. As she remembered bits and pieces of her dream, she tried to understand its meaning. Her grandmother told her dreams held a significance in our lives. Learning to interpret them was always a good practice. But fortune tellers weren't welcome in Parlimae Village. Lord Parlimae had outlawed them long ago.

She didn't understand who the violinist was. It wasn't her. The violinist had blonde hair, while hers was auburn. And she was just as mystified by the location of the village. It wasn't Parlimae—she would have recognized it.

As she looked around the valley, she remembered the trees in the background of the dream. The village had been surrounded by a forest not unlike this forest. She couldn't be certain—there were many trees in this valley, including the thick pine grove next to the church—but this might've been the setting for her dream. Except the only thing here was the church and cemetery, no village in sight.

"Ally? Ally?" Seth's voice snapped her out of her thoughts. She looked over at him and smiled. "You sure you're OK?"

She nodded.

"So," he said, "why?"

"Why what?" she asked.

"Why did you want to know if I remembered when we first came here and the dead road agents?" he asked.

She looked back at the flowers covering the iron gate, closely studying the poisonous thorns. "Do you think these flowers could have killed all the people here?"

"I don't know. Maybe," Seth said. "Definitely killed the highwayman. Is that what you are afraid of, the flowers?"

"No. Not really. I dreamt of a beautiful woman playing music in a small village. I think it was this village," she explained as she began to walk toward the church.

"Ally, there is no village here. It's just the church."

"Not now. But there was once. The church and cemetery weren't put in the middle of the forest all by themselves. There had to have been a town here. They're just all that's left of this forgotten place." She paused to look around the forest, imagining a village among the trees. "She was playing the violin and walking through the streets. She was dressed in a soft, white nightgown, but it was cold out, not the end of summer like it is now. It was nighttime and a full moon hung overhead. I could hear a howl off in the distance. And these . . . these flowers were growing as she played. Like she was having them consume the town."

"How'd you know it was cold out? In the dream," Seth said.

"I could see her breath," Alessandra said, drifting off in thought.

"What was the song?"

"What?"

"The song on the violin," he said. "What was the woman playing in your dream?"

"I'm not sure. But I recognized it. I knew it. I mean, I know it. I've heard the song before," she said, looking out over the valley.

"It was just a dream, Ally. Whatever happened to this place happened a long time ago," Seth said.

"I know. Maybe we shouldn't come here anymore. It's far from the castle. If anything were to happen. . ." She paused. "I think we should have told Lord Parlimae about the highwaymen. I mean, what were they doing here? Who were they?"

"I doubt anybody is looking for them. And nobody is going to look for them here. Nobody looks for the living among the dead. It's one of the reasons I like coming here with you; it's the only place we can be alone," he said. "Those two stumbled across this place just like we did. They were a couple of criminals who hurt people to get what they wanted."

"But when you found the shovels in the back of the church, there was a bed there. Maybe this was their place," she said.

"What? Like a hideout? Maybe, but the bed hadn't been used for a long time. And it didn't look like anybody used the fireplace either. Besides, if this was their place, they would have known about those flowers and stayed away from the gray vines. And who knows what killed the second guy. Could have been a fight or an animal attack.

"I don't think telling Lord Parlimae is a good idea," he said. "We'd have to discuss what happened in Mercel. It was almost a year ago. I know we don't get to come out here that often, but we haven't seen anybody around since that time. Maybe when William gets back from his hunting trip, we can talk to him about it."

Seth looked around, his face downcast. "Once we tell them, everyone will know it's here. It's the only place we can really be alone. We didn't kill them, or anybody else. Well, other than . . . you know. But they're laid to rest in a proper cemetery. There hasn't been anything going on here since that day. Wolves appear from time to time, but even they stay away from the flowers. We just have to be careful not to touch them."

Alessandra gave him a teasing smile and pulled him close. "But you love the smell of those flowers, remember?"

"Yes, I do." He kissed her, this time longer and with more passion.

Although she didn't want to, she pulled back. "We'd better get going. I have to be back before dark or my dad will be furious."

Seth smiled and said, "Once more, before we leave? You know what the smell of these flowers does to me."

Her smile widened as she giggled. "We can't or we'll never make it home before dark."

Seth gave a small grin. He loved her and always wanted to be with her. "I love how the aroma attaches to you. It's the only thing I like about going home. You smell so good as we are riding."

"Stop!" She giggled again, slapping him playfully on the chest.

"I meant riding home," he quipped. "But you're right. We should get back. I don't want your father getting upset and hunting me down. No need to cause a commotion."

Seth untied Boggs, his giant draft horse. He cupped his hands together for Alessandra to use as a step. "Besides, I don't think he likes me very much," he said as she swung her leg over the horse.

"He likes you just fine. He's just very protective of me," she said, sliding back to give Seth enough room to jump up. He grabbed a handful of the horse's mane and pulled.

A small click of his tongue told the gentle giant to start home. Alessandra laid her head on Seth's shoulder and held on tight. There wasn't any worry about falling off. The horse didn't move that quickly, and its back was very wide. She just liked being close to Seth one more time. The ride home was always bittersweet. She got to cling to Seth, but it marked the end of a magical time.

She looked over her shoulder at the abandoned church as they trotted away, starting up the hill out of the valley. She could imagine the former village more clearly than ever before. Despite the trees and overgrowth that hid the location of the old buildings, the village's layout was clear from this viewpoint, thanks to her dream.

Alessandra, Seth, and Boggs

She thought about the dream the whole way home. The sound of Seth's heartbeat seemed to harmonize with what she could remember of the violinist's song. But it was all flashes in her mind, as she couldn't exactly remember the end. She could see her hand spinning the violinist around but couldn't see the face. Then again, maybe that hadn't been her hand. Perhaps it was someone else's hand, and this vision was just a way for her to witness something. But what? The dream seemed both wicked and beautiful at the same time.

Seeing the old village in her dream reminded her of the first kiss she'd shared with Seth. It started with an unexpected adventure.

Almost a year ago, William had stopped by Alessandra's house early in the morning. His father's guards were slowly riding through the village, escorting a couple of wagons to Port Calibre. They were tasked with transporting Lord Parlimae's shipment, which had arrived by boat a few days ago. Lord Parlimae had asked William to go with the guards.

He was older now and expected to take life a little more seriously. Indeed, all three of them had earned more responsibilities. The days of wasting away the afternoon while fishing had come to an end. Life was more than swimming in the summer and gathering wood for the winter. Well, she and Seth had gathered wood; William did very little.

But the lord of the manor had started asking more of his son, which was how he ended up at Alessandra's door that morning. Her father greeted William with a big smile. "Good morning, my lord. What can I do for you? Care for a warm beverage? Perhaps some breakfast?"

"No, no. Thank you. I'm just here to see Alessandra," William said.

"Of course, of course. Let me get her," her father replied before leaning inside the house. "Alessandra! Could you come here, Daughter?"

"Yes, Papa." She yelled back as she came through the house.

When she saw William standing at the door, she smiled in greeting. "William? Hi. What's going on?"

"Father has asked me to see to a shipment coming from the port. I thought you might like to come along." William had exaggerated his

William

father's instructions. Lord Parlimae had merely told his son to accompany the guards so William could learn more of the duties that were often required of the lord of the manor. He would never have trusted such an important shipment to William's charge.

A boat dealing in black market goods had come across a special relic. This item had been intercepted on its way to Rome. Some of Lord Parlimae's road agents had been dispatched to intercept the shipment, but they'd disappeared suddenly.

Lord Parlimae hadn't told William about the item or its importance. With the disappearance of his men, he decided subterfuge was in order. Sending his son would be less suspicious to anyone who may have learned of the relic. Nobody would believe the lord would send his son on anything of importance. And Lord Parlimae did not know that his men had died. To him, it was the perfect camouflage.

William wasn't very well respected. He was seen as a bumbler of sorts. Nobody challenged him because of his father, but William did not know this. In his mind, he was both suave and feared.

"Well, that sounds important. And your father put you in charge of getting this shipment back?" she asked skeptically.

"Alessandra, I am sure the young master is quite capable of handling such an important task, whatever it may be, or Lord Parlimae would never have entrusted him with it nor allowed him to request his friends join," her father said.

She knew how Lord Parlimae regarded his son, and she was naturally skeptical of William's description of his duties. Regardless, they were still friends, and she was all too happy to get away from her chores for the day. "Does that mean I can go, Papa?"

"Of course, Daughter. Be home by sundown. There's much to do yet this year," her father said with a smile. "You will take good care of her, young master? Have her back by dark?"

William nodded. "Yes, sir. I surely will."

Alessandra stepped out, shutting the door behind her. "Is Seth coming?"

William shrugged slightly, ignoring the question. He had no intention of inviting Seth. This was his chance to be alone with her. She had yet to notice the way he looked at her. William had developed strong feelings for her. Unfortunately for him, they only flowed one way.

His father noticed it. That was another reason he gave William more assignments beyond the village. Lord Parlimae loved Alessandra. She was the daughter he'd always dreamed of, but she was not suitable for William. Lord Parlimae needed to turn William's attention to someone with a more suitable lineage for a proper marriage. He did not realize that it was too late.

"I'm not sure where Seth is," William said, climbing into the saddle of his horse. "I haven't seen him. I don't have time to look for him this morning. We must stay with the wagons. You still want to come, don't you?"

She nodded, visibly disappointed that Seth would not be coming. She didn't like riding with William, who constantly attempted to prove his masculinity by riding fast. Plus, she wasn't comfortable holding on to him. They'd been friends for years, but her feelings hadn't progressed like his had. But this seemed like the only way, so she took his hand. He pulled her up behind him.

William was handsome and well built. Most women would've done anything to be with him. There were rumors some may have. Anyone bearing his child would have enjoyed a much easier life. Alessandra didn't believe the rumors about him sleeping with some of the wives in the village. Others, however, knew the stories were true.

William had many affairs, and not just with villagers. The wives and daughters of visiting dignitaries were known to receive a late-night call from him. But none of them captured his heart like Alessandra. They were just objects to be conquered and to satisfy his lustful ways. And none were as beautiful as she.

There was nobody in the entire valley as pretty as Alessandra. Nor was there anyone as sweet or as kind—or in possession of such a strong work ethic. She was the perfect bride, someone to take care of his every need. Even if she didn't know it, William intended to marry her.

William suspected his father did not approve of his desire to marry Alessandra, which confused him. Lord Parlimae seemed close to her family. At least as close as a lord and his subjects could be.

He often saw his father speaking with Alessandra's grandmother while her dad was in the fields. Lord Parlimae had even invited her grandmother to be his official tailor. He'd seemed hurt when she turned down the offer, citing her wish to stay closer to her family.

William was feeling good about today despite the issues with his father. He hadn't told Lord Parlimae he intended to take Alessandra with him. He knew his dad would somehow ruin his plans, and this seemed like an opportunity to spend a lot of alone time with her.

But as they were approaching the outskirts of town, Alessandra spotted Seth. He was watering his draft horse at the edge of the village. She waved to him and called out, "Seth! Seth!"

He turned to see her riding with William and shivered at the look that crossed William's face. It was an expression he wore when hunting, just before he shot something: subtle and devious, with an evil grin.

Very few people ever noticed it. Alessandra didn't see it until she was much older. Back then, she had yet to learn how to recognize those little things in people. She hadn't even noticed the way William looked at her.

Maybe that was because she had fallen in love with someone else. She may have not recognized William's glances, but she noticed everything about Seth. All his micro-expressions captured in her brain. She didn't know how to interpret most of them, but she did pick up on them.

And now it seemed like something was off, even though Seth smiled wide and waved back. It wasn't the hearty, happy wave she was used to seeing. Was he jealous because she was on William's horse? She liked that thought.

William, on the other hand, didn't like any of it. But he didn't have much of a choice. He stopped when they reached Seth and was surprised when Alessandra slid off his horse. She had a bounce in her step as she walked up to Seth.

"Lord Parlimae has put William on an important mission. Come with us," she said.

Seth looked up at William, whose expression had changed. He no longer looked upset. The last thing he wanted was for Alessandra to see the darker side of him. "Yes, grab your things and come along. Unless you have chores to do or something," William remarked.

Seth looked at him skeptically. William's face was friendlier, but Seth had known the boy his whole life. He wasn't sure if William really wanted him to go, no matter his insistence.

"C'mon," William said. "You can catch up with things later. It'll be fun. The three of us haven't been on an adventure in a while."

"I shouldn't." No sooner had Seth said the words than Alessandra started pouting. Her back was to William, which was fortunate for Seth. If William had seen the look in her eyes when she saw Seth, he may not have been able to handle it.

Seth looked back at the fields, then patted his big horse's neck. "OK. I guess it won't hurt anything. Shall I grab my musket?"

"You won't need it. The castle guards will be with us. Besides, we don't have time. We need to catch up to them," William said.

Alessandra let out a small squeal of excitement. "I'll ride on Boggs," she told William, impatiently waiting for Seth to help her up on the mighty horse. "There isn't enough room on yours."

Neither Alessandra nor Seth knew it, but that was the moment when it all started. The smallest spark sometimes causes the biggest fire. Two were lit that day. It was the exact place and time when Seth fell in love with Alessandra Moreau. It was also when William Parlimae began to hate them both.

Her intention wasn't to reject William. He had been generous to both her and Seth. Yet there was something about him that kept her from being attracted to him in a romantic way. Besides, she had already fallen for Seth.

William showed no signs of jealousy or animosity. He led them out of the village at a hurried pace to catch up with the wagons. The guards were moving slowly, but stopping to fetch Alessandra had put him behind schedule.

They crossed a wide field, stopping once for a herd of goats making its way to the southwest pasture to graze. They liked to gobble up the grass while the morning dew still sat on the blades.

Alessandra was wide eyed as she looked around. She held on to Seth a little tighter. Maybe it was the excitement of a new adventure, but something about this day was special.

TWO

WE THREE TO MERCEL

*I*t didn't take long to catch up with the wagons. The captain of the guard, Corsi, saw them approaching at a gallop and slowed his horse to speak to William. "Everything all right, Sire?"

"Quite fine. You may carry on," William responded.

Corsi raised an eyebrow. He didn't like it when William acted like a big shot. He didn't care for William at all, regardless of the fact that he was the lord's son. William often liked to portray himself as the man in charge, which was not the case. The captain was sure it was for the benefit of Alessandra and Seth, who rode up just in time to hear William throw his authority around.

Being an ill-tempered man, Corsi waited until the pair could hear his response before addressing William in a curt voice. "Your father didn't say anything about these two coming with us."

"They're with me. I think you should worry more about getting our cargo and the return trip than whom I invite along," William snapped.

"As you wish, Sire," Corsi responded, tipping his hat to Alessandra. "Do try and keep up, young sir. I shan't like to rescue you from another riding mishap."

With a snap of his reins, Corsi sprinted ahead, returning to the front of the caravan.

William's face turned red. His anger was barely contained. He looked over at Seth and Alessandra, who were pretending to have missed the captain's snide remark. But William knew they had heard, and it embarrassed him.

For now, his building resentment toward Seth was overshadowed by the captain's disrespect—in front of his friends, no less. William would neither forgive nor forget. He rode silently for quite a while, seething. His mind filled with plots to get back at the guard captain.

They followed the guards through the forest for some distance before coming to a split in the road. The path east went to Port Calibre, while the road west continued deeper into the forest. The wagon train came to a stop at the split. "What's going on?" Alessandra asked.

The wagons, along with the majority of the guards, turned east toward Port Calibre. Corsi and three of his trusted guards turned west.

Seth pulled his horse to a stop at the split. "Looks like the guard captain and a few others are going deeper into the forest," he said to William. "I thought we were going to Port Calibre."

"As did I. Wait here." William snapped his reins, racing to speak with the captain. Corsi did not stop as William trotted his horse beside him. "Why are we turning west, Captain? Is not the cargo being delivered by ship? Why are you not going with the wagons?"

Corsi pulled his horse to a stop. William halted beside him, then turned fully in his saddle. He saw Seth and Alessandra sitting atop their horse at the split in the road and, beyond that, the wagon train heading east. "We aren't going west. *I* am going west. You and your friends need to continue with the wagons. My men and I will be along shortly. Either that, or it might be a good place for you to go back to the castle."

"I told you. They are my guests and are coming with me," William said. "And *I* am coming with you, Captain."

"Very well. And as I told you earlier, keep up." Corsi leaned forward in his saddle, looking William directly in the eye. "You are not in charge here. You're a petulant boy. My job is to bring the cargo back as the master commanded. He saddled me with taking you along. I am sending the wagons to retrieve the cargo from the docks while I tend to other business. I'll catch up with them on the return trip."

"What business is that?" William demanded. "Does my father know about this?"

"Your father is aware of everything, boy," Corsi snapped. The other guards laughed.

William's anger grew. "Someday I will be the lord of the manor, dear captain. You would do well to remember that."

"That may be, Sire. But right now, your father has tasked me with seeing to this cargo as well as other business. Business you need not concern yourself with." Corsi threw a glance at Alessandra and Seth. "If I were you, I'd be more concerned about a peasant boy taking your girl."

"They're my friends. She's not my girl," William hissed.

"No? With the way you always look at her when she comes to the castle, I thought she was. I guess those old, lonely wives of the village are more your thing." Corsi smirked. "If she were my girl, I'd be damned before I let some farm boy take care of her. I wonder if the two of them will come with us or continue to Port Calibre together."

"Perhaps it is you who should not concern yourself with the business of a noble. We'll be coming with you," William said as he turned his horse, galloping back to Seth and Alessandra.

"What's going on? Where are they going? Where are we going?" Alessandra asked.

"The mission is very sensitive. I can't really say much right now. I've sent the wagons on to Port Calibre. The captain and I have other business to attend to. Seth, you should accompany the wagons to the sea. Alessandra, you can come with me if you like," William said.

Alessandra didn't waste a moment. "We're with you. Where you go, we go, as always. Right?" She said pinching Seth's side playfully. "It'll be fun."

Seth nodded reluctantly. William gave a small smile and turned his horse. He had hoped Seth would go east with the wagons. He was at least glad they didn't turn back altogether. It was a gamble telling Corsi his friends would be coming west with them. If Seth had decided to follow the wagons, it would have made him look like a bigger fool. William hadn't liked the idea of suggesting Seth go to Port Calibre alone—there was always the chance Alessandra would choose to go with him—but it had worked out.

Although William's mind rested a bit easier, he could feel pressure starting to mount. Alessandra's actions toward Seth had not embarrassed William in front of the captain, but Corsi's words had planted a small seed in his mind. A seed that was growing as they trotted along. William wanted Alessandra more than ever. He just needed a way to spend some time alone with her.

The guards moved faster now that the wagons weren't holding them back. Though the horses trotted at a quickened pace, Alessandra was still able to take in the sights and sounds of the forest. Neither she nor Seth—nor even William—had been this far west before, so everything was new. Rays of light came through the canopy-like pale-yellow curtains descending from the heavens. Green ferns shone brightly with radiance. The areas beyond the light were dark with foliage, fallen logs, and twigs.

The horses crossed a stream that meandered for several miles before reaching a small opening in the dense forest. A building to their right was tucked against some trees. It was hard to see at first, but once they noticed it, they started spotting more. The rest of the town slowly revealed itself.

There weren't many buildings here. Few trees had been cleared for the town. Houses and buildings alike were built into the forest, leaving most of the canopy intact. Some of the structures were even built around the trees themselves. Only the streets were void of obstacles. There was enough room for wagons to come and go.

It was a little damp here, the shade preventing the sun from drying the earth. Puddles were commonplace. Mud and muck had been churned up by the egress of horses. As they entered town, they spotted a big livery on their left, sitting just off the road. An alley led to the side of the building and ran parallel to the main road, all the way to the other end of town.

A small corral beside the livery enclosed several horses. The guards rode up to the building so they could dismount and tie their horses. Seth and William followed right behind them.

A small blacksmith shop was built to the side of the livery. The town smith was hammering heated metal on an anvil out front. The moment the guards pulled in, he stopped what he was doing and came out to greet them. Corsi flipped him a coin. "We won't be long. Keep our horses safe."

The blacksmith pocketed the coin and nodded as the guards grabbed their muskets.

William pulled his horse up to the corral, dismounted, and tied it to the fence, as did Seth. Alessandra got off the horse, then asked, "Where are we?"

"I don't know," Seth responded. "I didn't even know there was a town in the middle of the Dark Forest."

"We are in Mercel," William said. "It's not really a town."

Seth looked around. "Kinda looks like a town."

"It's not an official town." William gave their surroundings a sideways glance. "Mostly criminals here. It's not recognized by the monarchy. Not even sure the king knows about it."

As the three guards made their way into town, Corsi came over to William, Seth, and Alessandra.

"I would recommend you stay near the horses, but I know you have trouble obeying orders," he said with a pointed look at William. "So if you insist, stay close to us. Keep out of trouble. More important, stay out of our way. And stay out of the alleys. We shan't be here long."

Corsi didn't wait for a response. He hustled to catch his men before they got too far ahead.

Alessandra, Seth, and William hurried along but stayed well behind the guards. They wanted a better look at the town without being

rushed. While most of the homes on the main street had porches, those whose doors opened into the alley had none. The two side streets were behind the main street, with alleys connecting them.

None of the streets or alleys in this town were straight. Each wove around trees or giant rocks. Most were big enough for a wagon, but it was a tight fit. They hadn't been built for travel; they were created to help the residents move about quickly.

The guards were all business as they kept a watchful eye. The guard captain had caught up quickly, and the four of them led the way, all scanning for anything of concern. Occasionally they would look back to make sure William, Seth, and Alessandra were still with them.

The captain's words clouded William's thoughts. When the guards looked back at him, he swore he saw them chuckling to themselves. Except this was all in his mind. They were glancing back, but none of them were laughing. When he glanced over at Alessandra, he swore she had moved closer to Seth, another figment of his imagination. She was walking between both of them, but he didn't see it that way. His resentment continued to build.

What does he know? The captain is going to get what is coming to him. But not before he sees that she is here for me, not Seth.

As they passed the general store, a group of riders came thundering into town from the east, behind them. One peeled off, going into the stables, while the other two continued to the inn. This startled Alessandra, who instinctively grasped William's arm. He sneered at Seth. *I'm the one she wants.*

The riders directed their horses down the alley beside the inn and tied them to a post at the top of a set of stairs that descended belowground. Once the horses were secure, they went down the stairs and into the tavern.

The wooden door creaked and banged as they entered. It was early midafternoon, so no sound escaped the tavern. Only hard-core drinkers would be inside at this time of day. The music and laughter normally coming from such establishments wouldn't start until the sun went down.

"We're not going to make it back to the castle by sundown," Seth said.

"Maybe you should go back. I can take Alessandra home," William snapped. When Seth didn't respond, he gave another snide comment. "No? Then let's hear no more about it."

Seth gave a quick look to Alessandra. She lowered her head and grinned, careful not to let William see.

They followed the guards all the way to the inn. One of the guards remained outside near the front stoop. He would keep an eye on the town while the rest continued downstairs to the tavern. The first through the door was Captain Corsi, and the last was Alessandra.

"I've never been to a tavern, other than the Three Fields, that is," Alessandra said upon entering.

"It's early. Not much happening in here now, I suppose. You'll be fine. You're with me," William boasted.

She looked over at Seth, who didn't give a reaction. He'd learned long ago that William always noticed, even when Seth didn't think he was watching. His insecurities and distrust of everything around him kept a constant vigil.

The tavern was nearly empty. A few old-timers were standing at the bar, sipping ale. In the back, a man was shuffling a deck of cards. A strange-looking fellow sat at a table by himself. He wore a short cap that had a long feather tucked into the band and trailing out the back.

The moment Alessandra walked through the door, the dealer's eyes flashed yellow. It was so brief that nobody caught it. Except Seth. The dealer noticed the look on Seth's face, and he knew that Seth had seen.

Without a word, he packed up his cards. As the guards grabbed a table, the dealer stood up and quietly walked to the door. He stayed to the far wall, within the shadows, and was careful to avoid making eye contact with anyone. His movements were slow and deliberate to avoid arousing suspicion. He almost made it to the door before the innkeeper called out from behind the bar. "Oy. You comin' back to start da game, yeah?" She was a salty old woman who took no sass.

The dealer didn't look back. He turned his head to the side and tipped his hat slowly before grabbing the handle of the door.

"All right then. Make sure you're back by dark," the innkeeper said as the dealer left. She turned to the guards. "Got some players comin' in tonight. Don't want to disappoint me guests." She approached the table. "What'll ye have, boys?"

"Pints. And something to eat," Corsi replied.

"I'm the only aproner here today, love. Me and me son, that is. A bit early for any of my dashes, let alone da girls. They don't come in till tonight. You all might want to stick around." The old woman sighed as she wiped the table in front of them with a cloth. "Not much to eat yet, I'm afraid. Food's gettin' ready now. Cookin' an' bastin'." At the look on the captain's face, the innkeeper changed her tune. "But I'm sure we can whip some'n up for you gents."

The innkeeper turned to William, Seth, and Alessandra, who were seated at a neighboring table, near the wall. "What 'bout you three? Ales all around? You be wantin' some food as well?"

"I'll have an ale," William replied.

"Bit o' wine for the lady?" the innkeeper asked Alessandra.

"Yes, please," she said. "Bread maybe?"

"'Bout you? Ale or some'n else?" the innkeeper asked Seth.

"Brandy?" Seth half asked, half replied.

"All I gots is dis special dark. Bit bitter, you ask me." She raised an eyebrow, and Seth nodded in acceptance. "It's your nickel."

The innkeeper cackled while walking away, then called back, "Bread an' ale comin' up." She went behind the bar, yelling up a staircase behind it, "OY! GIT DOWN HERE AN' HELP YER MUM!"

She gathered a few pint mugs and began filling them with wine and ale. By the time she was done, a young man had come down the stairs. He grabbed the mugs when she disappeared into the kitchen.

The innkeeper's son served the guards first, then he brought William, Alessandra, and Seth their drinks. He was nearly back to the bar when the guards yelled out for more. Rather than retrieve their cups, he grabbed a pitcher and filled it with ale, then went to their table to refill their mugs. As he was finishing up, the old innkeeper returned from the kitchen, carrying some plates with charred meat and bread. She plopped a loaf on the table for Alessandra, Seth, and William, then put the tray of meat down for the guards.

When his guards were nearly finished with their food, Corsi moved to the rear of the pub. There were three men seated at a table just beyond the light. Neither Alessandra, Seth, nor William had paid much attention to them when they first came in.

These were the same men who'd rode into town earlier. The leader was a highwayman named Bouchard, a ruthless and cunning sort who didn't mind stealing what he wanted or cutting a man's throat—or a woman's. But thieving and murder weren't his primary concerns right now. For the moment, he was in sales.

"Do you have the item?" Corsi asked.

"Yes," Bouchard said.

"Well?" Corsi asked impatiently. "I haven't got all day."

"It's on its way. I'm afraid you'll just have to wait," Bouchard said sharply. He turned to look at Alessandra, Seth, and William before asking, "Who are your friends? A bit young, aren't they?"

"Never mind them. They are not your concern," Corsi snapped.

"Do you have what we agreed on?" Bouchard asked.

"*Oui*," Corsi responded.

"Well?" Bouchard said mockingly.

While Bouchard was certainly comfortable with murdering, Corsi was not a man to be trifled with either. He quickly snapped back, "It's not in the livery. Might as well send one of your lapdogs here to tell your man he can stop searching. And your men might want to take a look around before pulling those pistols."

Bouchard's eyes squinted. He and his men had been focused on Corsi and hadn't been paying much attention to the other guards. After eating and drinking, the guards had quietly moved to tables on either side of the room. None of that had bothered the highwaymen—Corsi had their full attention—until right this second. From those angles, the guards could kill each of the road agents with ease. And they outnumbered the highwaymen.

But that did not intimidate Bouchard. He had what Corsi wanted, so he had the advantage. "I'm afraid the terms of our agreement have changed."

"What?" Corsi's eyes moved slightly to the men seated with Bouchard. Their hands now gripped their pistols.

"The price is double. You didn't tell me what I'd be smuggling here. It seems this is quite the find," Bouchard said.

Corsi leaned in. "You weren't supposed to unwrap it. We said pristine condition."

Bouchard stood up slowly, putting on his tricorne. He casually walked over to the wall, pulled a lit candle off its holder, and pressed the flame to the bowl of his pipe. The flame revealed a long swath of skin marred by burn marks. He inhaled, lighting the tobacco.

He returned to the table and sat down next to Corsi, letting out puffs of smoke. "Your lord can well afford it. But I like the girl. Let's make an even trade for the surcharge. Our agreed price . . . and her."

Corsi glanced back at William, Alessandra, and Seth. Without any remorse, he said softly, "Fine. But not here. You take her later tonight."

Bouchard looked from the trio to Corsi. "And the two farm boys?"

"Sell them. Kill them. I don't care which. But they don't return," Corsi said. "Now, when do I get my hands on the item?"

Bouchard stood first, his men right after. "Later tonight. After dark."

"That wasn't the deal," Corsi snapped.

"Well, that's the deal now. Be at the livery after sunset. Wait till the moon is in the sky." Bouchard picked up his mug and chugged the last of his ale with loud gulps. The liquid dripped from the corners of his mouth. Using his sleeve, he wiped his face, then placed the empty cup on the table. "Don't be late. Bring my prize. She'll fetch a good price."

Bouchard walked toward the door with his men in tow. Before he opened the door, he paused to look at the trio. He said nothing but tipped his hat to Alessandra just before leaving with his men.

William, Alessandra, and Seth could see little of the man's face, aside from the scars. They couldn't hear his conversation with Corsi, so Seth and William thought he was being polite by tipping his hat. But Alessandra gave a sudden shiver. She saw the look in his eye, and it was creepy to her.

Corsi and his men got up to leave. One of the guards tossed some coin to the innkeeper. Corsi walked over to the trio. "We can't leave just yet. We need to wait a few hours. Then we'll go."

"A few hours? It'll be dark by then. We can't ride the forest road at night," Seth said.

Corsi stared down at him, then the others. "It will be fine. You are with Parlimae's finest guards. We are simply waiting for an important item for Lord Parlimae. Once we have it, we'll be off. You three stay here. One of my men will come and get you when we are ready to leave."

William was immediately suspicious. The moment the tavern door swung shut behind Corsi, he said, "The captain has been telling me this whole trip to send you two home. If we left now, we'd be halfway home by nightfall, and he knows that. All of a sudden, he wants us to stay."

"I thought you were in charge of this mission," Seth said.

Blood rushed to William's cheeks, but neither Seth nor Alessandra could see his flush of embarrassment in the dim light. "I was to lead them to Port Calibre, but when Corsi and his men turned to come this way, I insisted on accompanying them to protect my father's interests. He's up to something."

"Wait. I thought. . ." Seth started, but William cut him off. "We're here now. I say we keep an eye on them. I'd like to know who they were meeting with."

The innkeeper came over with a refill of ale and brandy. Before she finished pouring, Alessandra placed her hand on the old woman's arm. "Tell me, who was that meeting with our guard captain?"

The innkeeper pulled away slowly. "I really can't say, young miss. Probably castle business of some kind, I imagine. None of my concern. None yers either, I should think."

"Well, this is Lord Parlimae's son. I would imagine whatever business this is, it's his, wouldn't you? Unless we should let the lord know you so rudely refused to answer the question," she said.

The innkeeper swallowed, looked around to make sure the few people left in the tavern couldn't hear, then decided to answer. "All right, young miss. No need to be like that. The man's name is Bouchard. A highwayman. You know, road agent of sorts. He and his men are known to run back and forth through the western part of the forest. Best to take yourselves back east and home, if you ask me. Not the sort to be messin' around with."

With that, the innkeeper waddled back behind the bar.

Alessandra stood first. "Well then? You guys coming or not? Let's go."

William and Seth looked at each other, then followed her out of the tavern. Seth made sure the door didn't bang as they left.

Sundown was still a few hours away. Townsfolk ambled about. The three of them moved to the back alley, where they waited for dusk. When the sun had just about set, they made their way to the main street in search of Captain Corsi and his men.

Activity in the streets was dying down as darkness approached. People crossed the thoroughfare, finishing the day. Most of them were closing businesses, like the livery and general store. Riders entering town arrived at a slower pace in the failing light.

Bouchard exited a nearby building before Corsi and the guards. He gathered his man at the livery without anyone noticing. "Is it here?" he asked.

"No. Nuffin," the man responded.

Bouchard looked back at the inn. "Three will come out of the tavern. We want the girl. She'll fetch a nice profit in the slave trade. They should be out at dark. For now, let's get some rest."

Bouchard and his men decided to nap until it was totally dark. They bedded down in some stalls filled with hay. The blacksmith's hammer clinked at a steady rhythm that made it easier to fall asleep.

The noise from the smithy ended when the blacksmith left for the day. The silence signaled to Bouchard that night had come and it was time to meet with Corsi. He and his men emerged from the stables quietly and moved to watch the main street. The moment they were outside, Bouchard spotted Alessandra, Seth, and William, who were emerging from the alley next to the inn.

"That her?" one of his men whispered.

"That's her," Bouchard said quietly.

"And what about those two?" his man asked.

"Kill them," Bouchard replied.

His man's eyes lit up. "Wait, is that. . ." he mumbled more to himself than to anyone else. "I think it is."

Bouchard took a better look but didn't understand the man's excitement. "Who?"

"The big, dark-haired one behind the girl," he answered.

"What about him?" Bouchard asked.

"That's Lord Parlimae's son!" his man exclaimed quietly.

"I didn't recognize him in the tavern. But I see him now." Bouchard leaned back, contemplating what Corsi had told him. Softly, he said, "It would seem the good captain wants us to do some of his dirty work. I'm thinking the boy may get us as good a price as the girl."

He glanced at his man, then turned back to the trio. "After Corsi gives us the money, we kill him and his men. The girl gets sold on one of the slave ships in Port Calibre. Then we take the young prince and the item to Lord Parlimae. See how much they are worth to him."

"And the blond?" his man asked, referring to Seth.

"Him we kill," Bouchard said, smiling.

THREE

THE DEADLY RED DOOR

*A*lessandra's plan was for her, William, and Seth to watch Corsi and the other guards. It never occurred to her that the trio might be watched too. Bouchard and his men had spotted them as they left the alley, and when one of the highwaymen recognized William, thoughts of increase in coin began dancing in their minds.

But Bouchard had also underestimated his foe. He didn't think Corsi and his men were clever enough to watch the highwaymen while the highwaymen were watching the trio.

None of the highwaymen noticed Corsi's guard spying outside the inn earlier in the evening. Tucked behind an alley and out of sight, the guard had watched Bouchard and the highwaymen leave the tavern and then go to the stables, where they'd searched unsuccessfully for the coin trunk and taken a brief nap. When Corsi and the other guards exited the tavern a short time later, the guard relayed what he had seen to his captain.

They decided to find a place to wait until the sun went down, just as Bouchard was doing. The general store seemed like a good place. From the second-floor window, there was a good view of the main road. When the sun went down, everything became a little harder to see, even from that spot.

"What do you think, Captain?" one of the men whispered.

"I'm not sure. That impotent little shit can't do anything he's told. I'm guessing the three of them are looking for us." Before he settled in

upstairs, Corsi had watched Alessandra, Seth, and William come out of the tavern. The three had disappeared down the back alley, which shielded them from his view. As darkness covered the area, he saw them walking from the alley to the main road.

His men saw them too. "Should we go round them up?" the guard asked.

"No. Let's see what happens. The priority is the item. What happens to William is on him," Corsi said.

"What about Lord Parlimae?" the guard asked.

"Let me worry about our dear lord." Corsi had not told his men about the side deal he made with Bouchard for the girl. As far as they knew, Corsi was too focused on the item to care what happened to William or his friends.

He continued to watch as the boys caught up to Alessandra, who was leading the way. She kept to the shadows of the homes and businesses on the main street. At each crossing, she stopped and peeked around the corner. When the coast was clear, she picked up her dress and ran across the road to the next building. William was behind her, and Seth brought up the rear.

After they crossed an alley, they disappeared under a porch roof. Corsi's perch on the second floor obstructed some of his view. He could only see their feet as they walked along. When they came to another alley, he could see them again.

Bouchard and his men were on the street, watching Alessandra, William, and Seth move through town. In an attempt to remain unseen, the three stayed close to the front of the buildings. Likewise, the highwaymen retreated into the shadows to hide their positions. They moved through the dark alleys that ran alongside the homes to get a better view.

Corsi believed Bouchard and his men were scattered somewhere near the livery. He caught glimpses of them as they darted around, changing positions to stay hidden.

He hoped they would grab William and his friends quietly. Mercel didn't have a lawman, but the townsfolk looked after one another. While gunshots or sounds of a fight weren't uncommon here, they always drew a crowd. The last thing he needed was for someone to rescue them—or worse, send word to Lord Parlimae.

His hopes were dashed when William pulled a small pistol from his waistband. William followed Alessandra across the street to an alley. As he looked around nervously, he cocked the hammer. It wasn't a big pistol, but it would make the kind of noise Corsi didn't want.

He hadn't known William was carrying a weapon. Neither he nor Seth had brought a musket with them. Corsi expected a knife or two, but not a pistol. This would complicate things, especially if William was lucky enough to kill Bouchard before Corsi and his men got the item.

"Cap'n, look." One of his men had spotted the pistol too.

"C'mon. We'd better get down there," Corsi ordered. The guards quietly made their way down the back stairs. The owner of the general store trusted the castle guards, so he and his clerk had already left for the day, leaving the guards alone inside. This allowed Corsi and his men to go out the front door unnoticed.

As the men were leaving the shop, Alessandra was crossing the thoroughfare toward the alley that ran parallel to the main road and connected to the livery. As before, William was right behind her, still holding the pistol, and Seth followed.

Alessandra stepped into the alley, while Seth and William stopped at the corner. She turned to whisper, "We should have seen them by now. Stay here. I'll go to the end of the alley and see if there is anything on the back road. I think it goes all the way to the livery."

"No! Wait!" Seth's voice was hushed, but his words were emphatic. He tried to step around William.

William put his arm in front of Seth to prevent him from going into the alley. "She'll be all right. Let's just wait here for a moment."

Alessandra rolled her eyes, then whispered, "Just stay here. I'll be right back. Keep an eye out and make sure nobody sneaks up on you."

The rear of the alley had almost no light under the canopy of trees. Not even the moon's rays penetrated the thick foliage. The entire village was dark despite the moon. Seth and William did not see Corsi or his guards peeking at them from behind the general store. And nobody noticed Bouchard's men hiding in the shadows like predators waiting for the right moment to strike.

Alessandra walked to the end of the alley to get a better look at the back road. The boys could see most of her white dress. But once she reached the end, they lost sight of her in the darkness.

Seth was growing impatient. The moment he could no longer see her, his nerves began to fray. He wanted William to start down the alley, but William was not a brave man. He was a typical bully, full of insecurities and fears. Even though he was the one holding the pistol, he had no intention of going down that alley.

Several moments went by with no movement. Seth couldn't take it anymore, pushing past William so he could find Alessandra. William tried to grab him, but Seth had already made it through. William stayed put while Seth walked slowly toward the darkness, whispering her name. "Ally! Ally!"

She turned when she heard Seth's voice calling to her. She was just about to reply when a hand reached around from behind her and covered her mouth. It was one of Bouchard's men. With his other hand, he wrenched her arm behind her back. The move was so quick that she didn't have time to react. He dragged her down the alley, ignoring her muffled cries for help.

The pain and fear were overwhelming as she struggled to break free. She tried to scream, but his grip was too strong. Those big, meaty fingers and sweaty palms prevented her from calling for help. The more she struggled, the more he twisted her arm and squeezed her mouth shut. Nothing was stopping this brute from imposing his will on her as he dragged her to the livery.

Seth heard the scuffling and noises. He thought he caught a glimpse of Alessandra's white dress, but there were no signs of her. He feared something may have happened to her.

He couldn't see much in the dim light. He thought he'd heard her footsteps, but the sound of shuffling was muffled and getting fainter by the moment. When he reached the end of the alley, he looked in both directions. *Which way?*

Dealing with his own fear was a lot, but he was determined to find her. His heart raced, beating so loudly that it interfered with his hearing. But there was no mistaking the footsteps coming at him. By the time his mind registered what they were, it was too late. CLUNK! That was the last thing he heard before blacking out.

One of Bouchard's men had struck Seth on the back of the head with a wooden club. The assailant wasted no time flipping him over his shoulder and carrying him to the livery. The highwayman slid the livery door open and stepped inside with Seth over his shoulder. Bouchard closed the door and then grabbed a fistful of Seth's hair, lifting his head. "You idiot. This is the wrong one."

Bouchard's other companion, the one who recognized William, approached from the back of the livery. He took a look at Seth's face. "Oy, that ain't him."

Alessandra had been tied to one of the posts. Her eyes widened at the sight of Seth. Her mouth had been gagged, but she managed to give a muffled scream while struggling to break free.

Before she could get too loud, Bouchard's man was on her. He jabbed the point of his knife against Alessandra's throat. It wasn't enough to pierce her skin, but it was still painful. "Shut yer damned mouth. You ain't worth that much." He sneered. She could feel his breath on her neck. He groaned while sliding his slimy tongue up the side of her neck to her ear. She froze, nearly vomiting from the putrid smell coming from the man's mouth.

Bouchard let go of Seth's hair and drew his pistol. He aimed it at the man terrorizing Alessandra. Looking down the barrel, he called out menacingly, "You keep off her. She's worth more intact. The black ships pay a fortune for ones that ain't defiled. Now back off!"

The highwayman stopped, turned his eye to Bouchard, but didn't move. That wasn't good enough for Bouchard. He took a step toward the man, cocking the hammer of his pistol. "Or I'll put this right through your eye!"

The highwayman didn't like it, but he could see Bouchard wasn't bluffing. He pulled the knife away from Alessandra's throat and took a step back. He slowly raised his hands, holding the knife lightly. "OK, OK. No need for that."

But he couldn't help himself, turning his head to Alessandra with a wide smile. "With what we will get for you, I can spend an entire week in one o' them brothels. Maybe head up to Paris and enjoy one of them fancy ones. Get me a couple girls."

The highwayman who held Seth called to Bouchard. "What'll we do wit dis one?"

With his man away from Alessandra, Bouchard uncocked his pistol and tucked it beneath his waistband. "I don't care. Throw him in one of the stalls and keep him out of the way. We'll deal with him later. Maybe sell him too. He's strong. Might get something for him."

The young lord was the one Bouchard wanted, though he didn't know William was still where Seth had left him, looking down the alley. William was just about to go after Seth when he heard a creak behind him. He turned swiftly, pointing the pistol at the sound.

"Whoa! Easy, young master." It was Corsi. "What are you doing out here? I thought I told you to stay in the tavern." Corsi squinted past William and down the dark alley. "Where are your little friends?"

"They went down there," William said.

"Well then, what are you waitin' for? You better go find 'em," Corsi said.

"What about you and your men?" William asked. "Where are your other two men?"

"Don't worry about them. We're comin' with you," Corsi said. "Lead the way."

William was afraid of many things, but the one thing he feared more than anything else was being recognized for what he truly was: a coward. He couldn't let Corsi or anyone else know he was afraid. Besides, with Corsi and the other guard by his side, he became more empowered. William took a few cautious steps before moving faster down the alley. When he reached the end, he stopped to look both directions down the crossing street. It was just as dark, and he couldn't see very far, but it was obvious nobody was back there.

Corsi and his guard came up behind him, looking up and down the alley as well. They couldn't see anything either and decided to let William determine their next move. "What now?" Corsi asked.

The livery was a few short blocks down the street. The trees had been cleared from around the stables, and moonlight flooded the area. This allowed William and the guards to see the rear of the building. The livery was big, stretching from the alley to the main street. The corral with the horses was around the other side and out of view.

William, Corsi, and the guard made their way down the back street to the livery. There were no windows, which prevented them from seeing what was going on inside. William didn't know exactly what had happened to Alessandra and Seth. He hadn't heard the scuffle. They had just vanished down this alley. But he believed something sinister was afoot. He didn't know Corsi had sold them out.

William crept up to the rear door—where Bouchard's man had dragged Alessandra—and tried to look through the cracks, but he couldn't see anything. There were muffled sounds, like the cries of a woman, coming from inside, so he pressed his ear up to the door. He could hear talking but couldn't make out what was being said. Beyond the livery, the town was quiet. This was his only lead.

"Go ahead. We're right behind you," Corsi said to William.

William opened the door quietly and stepped inside. He saw Alessandra tied to a post in the center of the livery, a knife-wielding highwayman standing near her, and Bouchard a few feet away. He immediately aimed his pistol at Bouchard. The highwayman reacted instinctively, drawing his pistol and aiming it at William.

William was so focused on Bouchard and the other man that he didn't hear the third highwayman throwing Seth into a darkened horse stall. Neither Corsi nor his guard heard the thump of Seth's body landing in the hay as they followed William inside the building.

A wide grin crept across the face of the man standing next to Alessandra. He took a step back to avoid the line of fire.

William might kill Bouchard, he thought. His grin widened. He would then kill William, and with Bouchard and William dead, the castle guards would make the exchange with him. He figured Corsi and the guards only cared about the relic, leaving him with the coin and the girl.

While the standoff was commencing, Seth started to regain consciousness. His vision was blurry at first. As it cleared, he began to see the highwayman lurking in front of him. Beyond the man's hulking form, were William and Bouchard, who were pointing their pistols at each other. He couldn't see Corsi or his guard behind William, and he couldn't see the highwayman standing near Alessandra. His gaze went straight to Alessandra, who was gagged and tied to a post. The sight enraged him.

Seth looked around the stall for something to use against the highwaymen. Anything. Then he found what he needed. Without a sound, he quietly crawled over to it unnoticed. As his fingers slowly gripped the handle, he saw Corsi step behind William.

The captain of the guard pulled out his pistol, cocked the hammer, and placed the muzzle behind William's ear. Seth couldn't believe what he was seeing. William was even more shocked to feel the cool metal on the back of his head. "Put it down, boy. Put it down," Corsi ordered.

William considered squeezing his pistol's trigger and killing Bouchard, but the moment he did, Corsi would fire. He thought about turning on Corsi, but he couldn't do it fast enough. Once his attention shifted, Bouchard would fire. Reluctantly, he pointed the pistol in the air and uncocked the hammer. Then he reached back, offering the gun to Corsi. Without moving his pistol from William's head, Corsi took the small gun.

"It's like that, then?" William asked.

Corsi grinned. "I told you. You're not ready to be lord of the manor. I'd say you never will be."

Instead of tucking William's pistol beneath his waistband, he aimed it at Bouchard. This surprised everyone.

Corsi's guard, who was still standing off to the side, now had his pistol trained on the highwayman who stood near Alessandra. Everyone was frozen in place.

Bouchard opened his palm and uncocked his pistol. "Easy. Easy. We still have a deal, right?"

William glanced over his shoulder at Corsi. "Deal?"

"Seems your captain of the guard doesn't want you around," Bouchard said.

"You have the item?" Corsi asked impatiently. "First the item. Then you can have the boy."

"It's right over there." Bouchard motioned with his head to the corner of the room. Some type of pole with a wooden handle protruded from beneath a thick, brown cloth. "Where's the coin chest? I held up my end."

A familiar click sounded from the shadows of the dark stall. The hidden highwayman had pulled his pistol, cocked the hammer, and aimed it at Corsi. Then they heard the second click. The highwayman had two pistols, and he aimed the second at the guard.

Corsi and his guard had no idea how many men Bouchard had hidden throughout the livery. At their alarmed expressions, Bouchard became cocky. He gripped his pistol, then aimed it at Corsi's stomach.

His eyes moved to William. "He sold you out, kid. All of you. After we get the money, I'm going to take you back to your daddy and see how much you are worth."

This was news to Corsi. He realized Bouchard knew William's identity. When he made the deal, he figured they would kill William and Seth without knowing who they were, thereby eliminating his problems. Now, he had to kill everyone here, but the odds had shifted away from him.

"What about the girl?" William asked, nodding to Alessandra, who was still tied to the post.

"The black ships pay a heavy purse for beauties such as her." Bouchard looked back at her with a sneer. "And she is beautiful." He turned to William again. "She's still intact? You didn't defile her, did you?"

Bouchard laughed. Like Corsi, he sensed William was not her man. His comment was a taunt. But his enjoyment didn't last for long.

A loud crunching noise rang out, followed by the spurting of blood. The sound was wet and intense.

No one expected to see drops of blood land on Bouchard and Alessandra, but that was just the beginning. Red drops hit William and Corsi too. They even landed on the other highwayman and the guard.

They froze at the sound of a groan coming from the darkness. It grew into an agonizing scream. Their eyes went wide as the highwayman who had been hiding in the stall emerged with three large tines poking through his chest.

Seth had stabbed him through the back with a pitchfork. As the man's body fell, Corsi squeezed the trigger, striking Bouchard in the head. The force knocked Bouchard back a few feet. When he hit the floor, the pistol he'd been holding bounced out of his hand. William saw his chance. He dove for the gun just as Corsi fired his second pistol. The shot missed its target.

William grabbed Bouchard's pistol, flipped around, and fired. The musket ball struck Corsi in the shoulder as he fled toward the back door. He let out a cry of pain as he ran down the alley.

While William and Corsi were exchanging fire, the highwayman near Alessandra was shooting Corsi's guard. His musket ball struck the man square in the chest. The guard fell back, dropping his pistol. The highwayman didn't wait around. He slid the front door open and ran out into the darkness.

Seth ran over to Alessandra. He cut her loose and removed the gag. She fell into his arms, sobbing. Raw emotions ran through her. The brutality of what she'd witnessed boiled over.

William hurried to the guard who'd been shot in the chest. He was still alive, but the fear of death shone in his eyes. He coughed a few times, spitting up blood. William looked at him with a morbid curiosity.

"What's this all about? What is that thing?" William motioned to the cloth-covered pole in the corner.

The guard tried to speak but was barely able to get the words out. He coughed up more blood. Shaking his head slowly, he rasped, "No idea."

"Where's the coin chest?" William demanded.

"There is no coin chest. The captain lied," the guard said as the last bit of life left his body. His head fell to one side. William laid the man's head on the floor. He picked up the guard's pistol and looked around the room.

He froze at the sight of Alessandra looking up at Seth with tear-filled eyes. She pressed her lips to his as if she couldn't quite believe Seth was still alive. She kissed him long and hard.

Jealousy and rage filled William as he watched. His mind formed thoughts in its unusual, twisted way. He wasn't fazed by the death or blood. Instead, he was consumed by the thought that Seth was stealing something that was rightfully William's. It was he who'd saved her. It was he who had brought the guards in here. It was he who had confronted Bouchard.

Speaking of Bouchard. . .

William became distracted when he realized Bouchard's body was not there. He had been so consumed with jealousy while watching them kiss that he hadn't noticed any movement. Bouchard was gone.

William looked back at his two companions, who were still embracing. His mind went right back to those vitriolic thoughts: What had Seth really done? He'd sneaked up behind a guy and stabbed him with a pitchfork—a cowardly act. Seth wouldn't have had to do that if he hadn't gotten himself captured. He was virtually useless. *And while I was battling with Corsi and Bouchard, he gets the girl.*

The sound of footsteps outside stopped his mind from spiraling any further. Someone was coming toward the livery through the alley. Was Corsi coming back with more guards? Maybe it was other high-waymen. Or perhaps it was Bouchard.

William forgot about Seth and Alessandra as self-preservation kicked in. He had become a target in this deal and would need a distraction if he were to escape alive. He looked at Alessandra and Seth again. She was crying, and he was comforting her. *If they want each other so bad, so be it.*

"Go out the front! Get back to the castle," William said.

"We're not leaving without you!" Alessandra yelled.

"C'mon, we go together." Seth's voice was a plea.

"It's OK. I'm right behind you. Get moving. I'll make sure nobody follows us," William said.

Seth reluctantly pulled Alessandra to the front door. William moved into a dark corner to ambush whoever might come through the back door.

Seth took a quick look out the front. The moon's light allowed him to see the horses and corral. The rest of the street was too dark, thanks to the tree cover, but he didn't see any movement. He took a step outside, Alessandra following right behind.

Seth leaned back inside and called to William. "Come on. There's nobody out here. Let's go!"

Seth turned and led Alessandra to his draft horse, who was still tied to the corral out front. He grabbed Alessandra around her waist and threw her over Boggs. With a fistful of the horse's mane, he swung up behind her.

William could no longer hear the footsteps in the alley. He looked to Seth, who was waving for him to come with them, then ran to his horse. Before William could mount his horse, two shots rang out. The booms were followed by the sound of projectiles whizzing past. Wood splintered off the fence post. Both shots narrowly missed him.

William ducked behind his horse, removing the pistol he had taken from the guard. Two riders were thundering down the main street toward them. It was hard to see in the darkness, but he aimed and fired. The blind shot missed, and neither rider broke stride. "GO!" he yelled to Seth.

Seth kicked his heels and snapped the reins. Boggs neighed, then burst down the road, his giant hooves clomping loudly against the dirt. Seconds later, the riders stormed past William in pursuit of Seth and Alessandra.

Boggs was in an all-out gallop, but he was a big horse. Seth knew their pursuers would catch up quickly unless he did something. The moment Boggs went over a small incline, Seth pulled the reins hard, directing Boggs into the forest. It was a risky move in the dark, but Seth had little choice. The small hill shielded them from the riders' view, and the darkness of the forest aided their escape.

He had only seconds before the riders came over the knoll. Jumping off the horse, he grabbed the reins and pulled the big horse behind a fallen tree. It was a few feet off the main path and big enough to hide them, if he was quick.

Alessandra jumped down, holding onto Boggs's nose to keep him quiet. They could hear the sound of the riders' horses getting louder and louder. A moment later, their pursuers raced past without hesitation. The hoofbeats faded until the forest was silent.

Alessandra and Seth breathed a sigh of relief. Then she remembered their friend. "What about William? We have to go back."

"We can't. I'm not going to risk losing you. You heard them. If they catch us, you'll be sold to the black fleet. Nobody ever comes back from that, Ally. William will be all right. If they wanted him, they'd have stopped for him instead of chasing us. It's you they want. We must get back to Castle Parlimae." Seth was determined, and he would not change his mind.

"What about Corsi? He's still out there. And he betrayed William," Alessandra said.

"There isn't anything we can do about that now. Lord Parlimae will know what to do. William can take care of himself," Seth responded. When she reluctantly nodded, he helped her back on Boggs.

Seth decided to walk in front of Boggs as they traveled through the forest. That way, he could help the horse navigate the undergrowth, walk over logs, and avoid anything treacherous. The ferns were about knee high, making it hard to see in places, especially at night.

"You aren't riding?" Alessandra asked. They had been running for their lives, but she was calm now and could think clearly. And she thought about how it'd felt riding with him. She liked having him behind her. His arms had wrapped around her body to guide the horse. It made her feel safe. But it was more than that. She hadn't been able to enjoy it when they were fleeing, but now she relished the memory and hoped he would ride with her again. She was disappointed when he decided to walk ahead.

"What's this?" Seth brought Boggs to a stop. He was looking at a patch of ferns that led to a row of trees. To the left, the trees went up a gradual incline to the top of a ridge. "Looks like an old path. Or maybe a road was here. What now?"

"I say we go up the hill. That way is north. Should take us toward the castle. The path to the right would lead back to the forest road."

Seth nodded, then clicked his tongue to coax Boggs in the direction they wanted to go. At the top of the small hump, they could see further into the distance. The road made its way up and down more small hills. They followed it slowly, trying to keep the noise down in case the highwaymen were nearby.

Before long, they reached a much larger hill. Seth wanted to ride up the hill in case something happened and they needed to flee. He grabbed a handful of Boggs's mane and swung himself up behind Alessandra. He couldn't see her whole face, but he caught sight of the small smile that creased her lips. This is what she'd been waiting for.

Seth directed Boggs up the hill and stopped when they reached the top. A large ray of moonlight illuminated the valley below. To their surprise, the light was shining on an old church surrounded by knee-high grasses. Beyond the church, a pine grove extended up another hill.

A cemetery surrounded by stone walls sat behind the church. The only access appeared to be two iron gates covered in enough red-and-black flowers to give the illusion of a red door.

Seth clicked his tongue, guiding Boggs down the hill in a slow, deliberate walk. When they got about halfway down, Alessandra pointed to the cemetery. "Look," she whispered.

The moon's rays illuminated two men lying awkwardly at the cemetery gates. Neither of them was moving. "I see them," Seth whispered.

He nudged Boggs forward, continuing down the hill. The horse carried them right to the church. The structure appeared as if it hadn't been used in years. At the side of the building, Seth jumped off the horse and tied the reins to a small tree. He caught Alessandra as she slid down. A tiny smile brightened her face while she waited for him to let go of her waist.

After an awkward pause, Seth let go of her waist. He motioned with his head to the cemetery. "Let's see what happened."

He led her to the rear of the church. Each time they came upon a window, Seth peeked inside to make sure the building was empty. Seeing no movement, he moved on to the next. Alessandra peered through the glass before following, just to double-check.

Finally, they reached the rear door. Seth stood there for a moment, listening for any sounds. The church was silent, so he continued on.

Seth and Alessandra looked around cautiously. The hills were motionless. The sounds of the night were loud and uninterrupted. Crickets and frogs sang songs that drowned the silence.

High grass grew between the back of the church and the cemetery. With nothing disturbing the forest critters and no activity in sight, Seth decided to check out the cemetery. He'd taken a few steps away from the church when an owl gave two quick hoots.

The abrupt sound startled Seth and Alessandra, freezing them in place. Realizing it was nothing to worry about, they continued to the cemetery. This close up, the red flowers covering the gates were lit by the moon and even more vibrant. "Look at all those flowers. From the hillside, I thought these were red doors," Seth remarked.

They could also see the two dead men more clearly from here. The first was lying facedown in the grass. His coat was torn to shreds. Blood and pink flesh seeped through. The back of his neck was ripped open, with a big chunk of skin torn away, a white bone sticking out, and his red muscles showing. He had been killed by some type of animal.

The man lying just beyond him was holding on to the gate, his fist still clutching the iron bars. Red thorns from the gray vines under the flowers had pierced his skin. An extreme grimace of pain was frozen on his face. He'd died in agony. A trail of dried blood ran from his palm down his forearm and to the ground.

"Are those the two from Mercel?" Alessandra asked. "Did this just happen?"

"It looks like they were trying to get inside," Seth said, leaning down to touch the first man. "The blood has dried, but only recently. The bodies are still warm."

"But the man holding the gate wasn't mauled."

When Seth took a step toward the gate to get a closer look at the man's hand, Alessandra grabbed him by the arm. "Wait. Look!"

She pointed to the flowers. Droplets beaded at the tips of the red thorns and glistened in the moonbeams. She could see the same coloration on the dead man's hand.

"It's those flowers. He died from them. They're poisonous," she whispered. "Look at the ground."

Small indents speckled the dirt below the gates, the pockmarks more plentiful where the flowers grew thickest. As they examined the vines, a drop of liquid dripped from a thorn and struck the ground. The dirt sizzled faintly, like bacon cooking in a pan.

Seth and Alessandra watched as the drop burned a hole in the ground. Smoke rose along with a sweet smell that wafted through the air. "Is that the flowers?" Seth asked.

"I think so. Beautiful. And it doesn't look like the poison dries. What are they?" Alessandra asked.

"I've never smelled anything like that. It's so nice," he remarked as if captivated by the aroma.

"Probably what those men said," she quipped.

"Are those the two highwaymen who were chasing us? I didn't get a good look at them in Mercel. Looks like something started chasing them. This one is grasping the iron bar like he was trying to get inside. The poison killed him before he could open the gate." Seth stopped and looked around. "I can't see any tracks in the high grass. And where are their horses?"

He paused, and a heightened sense of danger settled in. "We'd better go."

"We can't just leave them here," Alessandra said.

"Why not? They're criminals. They were trying to kill us—or worse, sell us. The hell with them," Seth said. "I think we should go. Whatever killed that second guy might still be around."

Alessandra tilted her head to the side and smiled softly at him. "Seth, they weren't raised to be criminals. I'm sure they didn't grow up wanting to be criminals. Whatever they became, they started out decent. They should be buried in a cemetery. Laid to rest properly. Besides, the blood has dried. Whatever killed them is long gone by now."

"What about their horses? I don't see them anywhere. You aren't worried about this place?" Seth said.

Alessandra looked around, but the place didn't frighten her. "It'll be OK. The horses probably ran off during the attack. Boggs will let us know if anything comes around."

Seth took a long, deep breath. He nodded slightly, then started to walk back to the church.

"Where are you going?" Alessandra asked.

"I can't dig graves with my bare hands. And we have to find a way to open the gates without touching the vines. Stay here. And don't touch anything. I'll see if there is something in that back room to help us open those gates."

Seth walked back to the church. The rear door was a little stiff, so he shoved against it with his shoulder, forcing it open. Boggs shuffled his feet and grunted at the sound as Seth burst through. A small amount of moonlight came through the windows and allowed him to see. An old bed was tucked in the corner. Across the room, a fireplace looked as if it hadn't been used in years.

Seth stepped through the far door and into the sanctuary. He was supposed to be looking for shovels and other tools, but he was curious. When he stepped behind the altar, the floor gave a strange creak. He bent down and moved his hands across the wooden floor until he found a small hole big enough for his finger.

"Seth! What are you doing? What's taking you so long?"

Alessandra's voice startled him. He caught his breath, then returned to the back room. She stood at the back door, eyebrows raised.

"I'm here. Just having a look around," he said, annoyed at her impatience. He ignored his curiosity about the sanctuary floor and returned to his search for the tools. He found a shovel and some rope, then left the church and untied Boggs. He led the horse to the cemetery entrance.

Seth tied the men's feet with one end of the rope. He tied the other end to Boggs's saddle. A few clicks of his tongue, and Boggs pushed into action. As the horse moved forward, the rope dragged the men away from the gate. Or *tried* to drag. While the man who'd been mauled moved easily, the man who gripped the gate barely budged.

Boggs pulled a little harder. The man's hand did not let go, and as Boggs advanced, the gate began to swing open.

Seth clicked his tongue once again, and Boggs pulled harder. With the sound of tearing flesh, the dead man's finger came loose. The gate was fully open, and the corpse had been dragged away with the first man. A few of the vines had come off the gate when the man's hand finally released its grip. The first two bars of the gate were now free of flowers.

Seth steered Boggs in a wide turn to move the bodies into a better position. He was careful to avoid the gate and patches of dirt that had held the bodies. He didn't want Boggs stepping in any poison that may have landed on the ground.

Boggs stopped, and Seth used the shovel to open the second gate so they could stay clear of the flowers covering it. Once both gates were open, he led Boggs into the cemetery, dragging the two dead men. The long vines that were still attached to the poisoned man's body trailed behind.

In the cemetery, Seth untied the rope from Boggs's saddle. Alessandra walked in, mindful of the vines and flowers. There was only one shovel, so Alessandra perused the grave markers while Seth dug the graves. It took him a while to dig, drag the bodies into the holes, and cover them with dirt.

When they were both in the ground and covered by loose dirt, he looked at Alessandra and asked, "Should we say something?"

"I think we've done what we should," she responded.

"All that and no final words?" Seth asked.

"I said they should be laid to rest in a proper burial, not memorialized." She made her way to the cemetery's exit but froze before the gates when she spotted movement on the hillside. Seth came up behind her and looked in the same direction. He, too, saw the movement.

Boggs shuffled his hooves nervously and let out a strong puff of air from his nostrils. All sounds stopped. The crickets and frogs fell silent.

A long, piercing howl broke the quiet. Its eerie reverb echoed through the valley. Then another. And another from the opposite hill.

The howls were coming from everywhere!

The wolves were on the hills all around them. Seth ran to the gate and wedged the shovel between the bars, using the tool as a lever to pull the gate closed in front of him. He grabbed the other gate in the gap he'd created in the greenery when he pulled away the dead man's hand. With a tug, he closed it. Using the rope, he carefully tied the two gates together, mindful of the thorns. Poison drops let loose, hitting the ground with a sizzle.

Alessandra held Boggs's reins to steady him. She stroked his muzzle to calm him, but the sounds were frightening. Each time a wolf howled, Boggs shuffled and showed the whites of his eyes.

After the gates were closed, the smell of the flowers got more intense. This seemed to lessen the howls. As the wolves stopped calling out, Boggs became calmer. It was as if the flowers somehow hid them from the wolves.

Alessandra and Seth could still see the beasts moving across the hillside like quick flashes of shadows. The creatures made their way to the bottom of the hill and circled the cemetery. Thankfully, the high stone walls prevented them from seeing Alessandra and Seth, and the flowers' aroma masked their odor.

At the top of the hill to the north, another wolf watched the valley. He was male and dark as midnight, with a bit of silver around his mouth indicated he had lived a long life. This was the leader of the pack. He was much larger than the rest and twice as vicious. From his viewpoint, he could see inside the cemetery.

Alessandra and Seth saw the big wolf's silhouette on the hill. Both swallowed hard. Seth gripped the shovel tightly; he knew that if they could see the black wolf, the beast could certainly see them. "Get on Boggs," he whispered.

"Boggs can't outrun them," she whispered back, unable to hide the fear in her voice.

"He can get you to the church while I fight them off," Seth whispered.

"No. I'm not leaving you. I'd rather die with you than live without you!"

"If we don't do something, that may just happen," Seth said.

Alessandra's gaze landed on the cemetery gates just in time to see a wolf race by. The movement was so quick that she almost missed it. She looked at Boggs, who wasn't shuffling any more. He was almost completely calm.

She could see more movement beyond the cemetery walls, but the negative energy was gone. The wolves circled the cemetery, but they didn't appear interested in attacking. A wolf stopped at the front gate and sniffed the ground. It took a few sniffs, then suddenly hopped straight in the air. It was as if the wolf had caught a whiff of something it didn't like. The animal darted away without a sound.

The aroma of the flowers was stronger than before, and Seth took a long, deep breath of the sweet, alluring scent. He and Alessandra could hear the wolves outside, but they didn't sound aggressive—there were a few grunts, some sniffles, and a couple cheek puffs, but nothing more.

Alessandra scanned the hill where they had seen the black wolf, but he was no longer there. She looked back to the gate, and jumped back in fright. A large, red eye peered through an opening near the top. She froze in place, not knowing what to do.

The black wolf was looking at them! Boggs's nerves returned when he saw the eye. He shuffled and let out a loud neigh. The black wolf pulled back and let out a loud grunt. The wolves in his pack lifted their heads, their ears raised high. They had heard Boggs too.

The black wolf stood tall and motionless for several seconds, staring into the cemetery with his red eye. He gave two quick yips, and they were gone. Alessandra scanned the forest. The wolves ran over the hill to the east and disappeared from sight.

"They're leaving," Seth said. "I don't think they could see us in here."

"The big one did. There was something strange about him," she said.

"What do you mean?" Seth asked.

"I don't know. He looked right at us through the hole. He knew we were here. He could see us. And they all heard Boggs," Alessandra said. She thought for a moment, then whispered, "It was like Passover."

FOUR

RETURN TO PARLIMAE

"$\mathcal{P}$assover?" Seth looked at her, puzzled.

Alessandra had a faraway look in her eye as she gazed at the flowers. "Yeah. Don't you remember when Father Gregoire visited last Easter and led mass? His sermon was about the Israelites putting lambs' blood on their doors so the angel of death would pass by."

Seth looked at her blankly.

"Seth! Don't you ever go to church?" She giggled.

"You think that old black wolf is the angel of death?" Seth questioned.

"I don't know. No. I mean, the wolves just ran off. Don't you think it's a little strange?"

"I think they can smell the poison in those flowers. That odor probably masked our scents. Maybe they thought we were poisonous like those vines," Seth replied.

"You're probably right," Alessandra said.

"I think we should wait a little bit before we head out. Let's make sure they're really gone." Seth patted Boggs on the neck a few times. "Good boy. Good job."

Alessandra and Seth kept a watchful eye on the hills around them. After a little while, Alessandra let out a small sigh and said, "I think we can go. Let's get home. We should head north toward the castle."

"OK. I'll get the gate." Seth walked to the gate and carefully untied the rope. He pushed each side open with the shovel, making sure he didn't touch anything. Alessandra grabbed a handful of Boggs's mane

and jumped onto his back. She walked him out slowly while Seth put the shovel back in the church.

When he came out, she said, "Aren't you going to shut the gates?"

Seth shook his head. "No. Might be better to leave them open in case somebody needs to get in there quickly—like us, if those wolves aren't really gone. I left the rope tied to the gate so it could be pulled shut from the inside if need be."

He jumped up behind Alessandra and clicked his tongue to get Boggs moving. They trotted up the hill, keeping a watchful eye as they headed in the general direction of the castle.

"What about William?" she asked.

"I hope he made it back by now. I guess we'll see when we get home," Seth remarked.

He snapped the reins to keep Boggs moving at a steady pace. The old road was easy to see with the rows of trees on each side and the ferns growing between them. A few logs had fallen, but Seth steered around them. He didn't have time to take it slow with the pack still out there.

It took a few hours, but they finally connected to the north branch of the forest road, at which point Boggs kicked up the pace. The sun was starting to come up as they reached the meadow at the foothills of Castle Parlimae. Farmers were already making their way to the fields, some herding livestock to pastures for grazing. A few waved as the pair rode by.

The castle looked majestic in the morning sunlight, its high spires gleaming brightly. The light glimmered against the white stones of its walls. When they hit the edge of town, Alessandra and Seth spotted people moving about in the village.

Seth pulled Boggs to a stop and slid down. He helped Alessandra dismount, then leaned in to kiss her. She blocked him with a quick hand to his chest. "What are you doing?" she asked.

"I, well. . . I mean, I thought. . . That is, I was hoping to kiss you." Seth's cheeks were red with embarrassment.

"Right here? Where everyone can see? Why not go into the Three Fields Tavern and make out in front of everybody? My dad is probably looking for me right now. Be a fine thing for him to find me like that after being worried sick all night. And if he sees us together without William. . ."

Seth wasn't sure what to do. She had kissed him when he cut her free in the livery, but now she backed away. Did she not want to kiss him? Maybe he'd misunderstood how she felt.

Alas, he reasoned, this wasn't the time or place to get into things. Their friend was still not back, which was weighing on her.

Alessandra's gaze caught on something behind him, and her eyes went wide. He looked over his shoulder. Across the field, guards and wagons were coming out of the forest. "Look," she said, pointing. "It's William! He made it."

They waited as William led the wagon train up to the village. He stopped beside Seth and Alessandra and dismounted. He motioned for the guards to go on to the castle without him. Alessandra ran up to William and gave him a big hug. He was taken aback at first, not sure what to do. His thoughts raced—perhaps he had misread her feelings.

She let go and stepped back next to Seth. "We're glad you're OK."

William grinned sheepishly, then looked at Seth. "Did you two just get back?"

"Yeah. Just a few minutes ago," Seth responded.

"What the hell happened? You should have been here for a while now," William said.

Alessandra was about to tell him everything—the dead highwaymen, the abandoned church, the deadly flowers, and the wolves—when she saw Captain Corsi and one of the guards from Mercel riding past. They were at the tail end of the wagon train. Corsi's arm was in a sling. She was surprised to see him alive.

Seth remembered the look on William's face when Alessandra kissed him in the livery. He knew that look, and he was seeing it on

William's face right now. She may not have noticed, but Seth knew William was bothered.

He decided to give his friend an abbreviated version of the story. "We gave them the slip along the road. Had to hide behind some fallen trees. They kept circling trying to find us. It took us a while, but we finally lost them and made it back. How'd you get away?"

William narrowed his eyes. He didn't believe the story. Not long after Seth and Alessandra were chased out of Mercel by the highwaymen, William came through the forest. He hadn't seen a trace of Seth, Alessandra, or the highwaymen. He knew they hadn't come back to the castle on the forest road. And if the highwaymen had been circling around, as Seth suggested, William would have run into them.

He decided to let it go for now. "I'll tell you later. Three Fields for a pint?"

"Sure. After dark, though. I need to get to my chores. I'm probably in enough hot water as it is." Seth could sense something was wrong but didn't know what. He gestured at Corsi. "You good?"

"Uh-huh. It's all sorted now. There won't be any more issues. I'll tell you later tonight." William smiled at Alessandra, then mounted his horse and kicked his heels against its sides.

They watched as he caught up with the wagon train, which was making its way back to the castle. Alessandra turned to Seth. "That was Corsi and the other guard."

"Yeah. I think we should keep the cemetery to ourselves for now," he responded.

"William is our friend," she said quickly.

"I know. But you heard them at the livery. Corsi not only sold out William, but he was giving us to those road agents too. We should wait to hear what William has to say before we talk about what happened in the forest."

Alessandra agreed. "See you tonight, then?"

Seth nodded, and as their eyes met, he found it hard to resist her pull. He loved those big, brown eyes, but he had to get to work. Besides, she'd stopped him from kissing her. He walked home in confusion.

His dad asked where he'd been, and his brother peppered him with questions over eggs and bacon. After a late breakfast, they went to the fields for a hard day's work, Seth's mind still on that kiss—and the embrace that never happened.

Alessandra's father was waiting at the front door when she came home. "Are you all right? I thought you'd be home sooner. I didn't expect you to be gone overnight."

He was a little angry but let it go quickly. He believed she'd been on an errand with William and felt comfortable with that thought, so she let him think it. While he never said it, her father hoped she would marry William. She wasn't nobility, but he saw how William looked at her and thought there might be a chance the young lord married for love, not title.

For a brief second, she had considered telling her father what happened. But Seth's voice was in her head. There was no telling how her dad would react. Besides, she was home and everyone was safe, except for a few others who were killed. She saw no reason to say anything more.

Her grandmother gave her a big hug and kiss when she came in. "Want me to make you some breakfast, dear?"

"Sure, Grandmama," Alessandra responded with a smile. She sat at the table as her grandmother moved about the kitchen, cracking eggs and frying apples. She sat quietly as her father ate his breakfast. When he was finished, he put on his coat and laced up his boots. "All right, I'm off then. Much to do today. You help your grandmother with the chores around here, yes?" It was more of an order than a question.

"Sure, Papa." She smiled.

Her father left, shutting the door behind him. The moment it closed, her grandmother sat across from her. "So," she asked with a wry smile, "how was your time with Seth?"

Alessandra blushed and lowered her head. "I wasn't—"

"Oh, you don't think me so old I can't see, do you? I still have eyes, you know. I see how he looks at you and how you look at him."

"Father would say William looks at me the same way," she responded.

Her grandmother got up and added some apples to the pan. She cracked a couple more eggs before speaking again. This time, her tone was humorless. "That one is no good."

"Grandmama! He's my friend. He's just a little spoiled is all." Alessandra delivered a chastising look, then quickly changed the subject. "What makes you think Seth was with us? I went with William and the guards."

Her grandmother snorted. "I saw you following William through the fields and into the forest on the back of Seth's horse." She spooned the eggs and apples onto Alessandra's plate as she waited for a response.

Alessandra looked up at her. "Did Papa. . .?"

"No, dear. Your father was busy in town when you left. I was in the backyard beating the rugs." Her grandmother smiled. "It's OK. You are allowed to fall in love with that boy."

As she thought about what her grandmother had just said, Alessandra gazed out the back window. Their house was on a small hill in the middle of the village, and their backyard had an unobstructed view of the fields and Dark Forest beyond. She looked back at her grandmother. "Love? I think I'm a long way from that, Grandmama."

Her grandmother leaned down and kissed her head, not pressing any further. "Eat your eggs, dear."

As Alessandra ate her breakfast and Seth was making his way to the fields for the day's work, William was following the wagons across the drawbridge and onto the castle grounds. He galloped in just as his father exited the large front door.

"Ah, my son. Everything OK? How was your journey?" Lord Parlimae asked, giving him a warm embrace after he dismounted.

William looked at Captain Corsi, who was walking his horse to the stables behind the other riders. Corsi nodded to Lord Parlimae in respect as he passed. Most of the wagons continued, each delivering cargo where it needed to go. The last wagon stopped in front of the castle steps, next to William's horse.

William walked over to the wagon and flipped the cloth off the relic so Lord Parlimae could see it. "Everything went well. I retrieved the item you wanted, Father."

Lord Parlimae looked at William in surprise. He turned to look at Corsi, who was nearly at the stable. "What about him? Any problems?" He gestured to the sling around Corsi's arm and the blood on his shoulder.

"I handled it. Everything is fine. You did send him for this, didn't you?" William asked with a bit of sarcasm.

Lord Parlimae blinked at William as if seeing him for the first time in a long time. His boy had grown. He wasn't just a naive kid or the spoiled son anymore. He'd sent out a boy, and a man returned. This was not Lord Parlimae's original intention. He had wanted William to join a company of guards in retrieving a shipment from Port Calibre and escorting it back. Corsi had been on a separate mission to retrieve the item. Clearly William had ferreted out that plan, and he'd somehow accomplished it. He was pleased with his son.

To keep the item from prying eyes, Lord Parlimae reached into the wagon and covered it with the cloth. "Take two guards you trust and discreetly bring this to the dungeon. I'll deal with it later. Don't make a big deal of it, and nobody will think anything about it."

William grabbed the item, careful to keep it wrapped in the cloth. Before he walked into the castle, he looked back at his father and said, "I don't trust any of them. It's why I'm still here."

Lord Parlimae watched as William disappeared inside. His boy, now a man, moved something so precious that every guard under his command, every villager in the town, would kill them both to possess it.

William took the item down into the dungeon, passing servants and guards at an unassuming stroll. Though he knew it was important, he didn't fully appreciate the value of it. The item was worth more than any riches his father had ever acquired. No amount of gold, silver, or coin could equal this single relic.

William placed the item in an empty cell used for storage. The most valuable thing in the castle leaned against a wall among piles of junk.

He left the dungeon and went straight to his room, just as he had done a thousand times before. The staff was used to seeing him come in late at night or early the next morning and expected him to sleep all day. The habit was probably why Lord Parlimae had asked William to store the item in the first place: No one would suspect he'd done anything out of the ordinary.

William woke up in late afternoon and joined his father in the dining hall for supper. They discussed the trip—or the parts William was willing to share. He didn't mention Alessandra or Seth, knowing his father would not approve. Lord Parlimae would've been especially displeased with his inclusion of Alessandra. He had already made it clear that William was to marry someone of noble birth, not a peasant girl, no matter how beautiful she was.

And while Lord Parlimae had nothing against Seth, he preferred that William associate with people more suited to his class. He also wanted his son to surround himself with people who would obey him and men who would be loyal to him. Lord Parlimae knew Seth was a good boy, but he also knew Seth was not a blind follower.

Which was why Lord Parlimae would've been especially upset if he knew Seth had accompanied William on his quest—and knew about the relic. Whenever William thought about telling his father Seth had been there, he hesitated, afraid Lord Parlimae would kill the boy. That would pave the way for William to be with Alessandra, but it would be only a matter of time before Lord Parlimae found out Alessandra was there too. And despite William's growing animosity, Seth was still his friend.

William watched his father eat, but his mind was elsewhere. He wondered how many of the guards knew there had been something special in the wagon. Corsi did, but he wasn't going to tell anyone about it. Not now, anyway. Only a few of his father's guards had been involved in the exchange with Corsi. And half of them were dead. Those who survived weren't going to talk.

There was the matter of the coin chest too. Corsi had denied having one, but William suspected differently. If Lord Parlimae found out they'd kept it for themselves, he would surely kill them.

William decided that it was best to keep the entire account to himself for the moment. It was best to simply bask in the win: He had retrieved the item and pleased his father, which he enjoyed.

He finished eating and got up to depart for his meeting with Seth and Alessandra.

"Where are you off to tonight?" Lord Parlimae asked, always curious about William's whereabouts when he could sniff out a fresh scent. Indeed, William often splashed himself with fragrance before visiting the tavern.

"Thought I'd head into the village this evening," he answered.

"Take a few guards with you."

"I can take care of myself," William snipped.

"I know you can, my son. But there were some reports of wolves in the land while you were gone," Lord Parlimae said.

"I was only gone one day, Father. It wasn't that long."

"I know. Last night, word reached my ears."

"What are they doing? The wolves, that is. Killing livestock? People?"

"Just livestock for now. Witnesses described a very large pack led by a giant black wolf. Rumors are spreading about the return of the Beast of Gévaudan. People are afraid," Lord Parlimae responded.

"I'm sure there is nothing to worry about. Wolves won't come into the village." William walked out of the dining room before Lord Parlimae had a chance to respond. The castle doors slammed behind him, the sound echoing through the big hall.

William strolled into the courtyard as evening fell. The torches around the castle wall provided plenty of light for him to see as he made his way through the front gate. The moon was just a sliver against the thousands of stars that dotted the night sky.

He followed the line of torches over the drawbridge and into town. Candles twinkled in every window, and the villagers moved about in the warm evening air. It didn't take long to reach the Three Fields Tavern, which was located on the main street, only a few roads down from the drawbridge.

A wooden sign hung out front, proclaiming the tavern's name in big letters above the carving of a horse pulling a plow.

Outside, the sound of merriment was muffled, but William could tell everyone inside was having a great time. The pub door squeaked as he entered, though he could barely hear it over the noise. The sound of music and raucous laughter spilled out onto the street.

Three Fields was a big tavern compared to the others in town, one of which wasn't even a proper tavern. It was more of an underground room with ale. But this was the biggest and liveliest.

Lord Parlimae helped finance it to keep the villagers happy. He had loaned the owner funds to turn an old storage building into something his guards could visit too. There were prostitutes, gaming tables, and musicians. A big kitchen served meals all day, starting with breakfast. When the harvest was good, the proprietors would feed the poor folk in town. Lord Parlimae himself was known to visit from time to time. Reportedly, the potato and leek soup was a favorite of his.

Everyone stopped and looked as William entered. This was something he enjoyed. He wasn't smart enough to understand guests stopped to gawk at everyone who came in. William always wore his finest clothes when he came here. His deep red coat and matching cap—with its long pheasant feather spilling out the back—stood out in a crowd. He wore a white shirt with ruffles in the front and left two buttons open to show off his hairy chest. Spit-polished knee-high boots completed the look.

Nearly everything he wore was crafted by the town's best seamstress, which happened to be Alessandra's grandmother. A fact he also enjoyed. The sadistic side of him relished the idea that she was somehow a servant to him.

William was the very definition of a peacocking male. He was confident and self-assured everywhere he went. He believed the looks and whispers were signs of respect, adulation in the face of his magnificence. In truth, everyone knew he was Lord Parlimae's son. Those who didn't were not from the village and were quickly informed.

Half the peasantry feared Lord Parlimae, thereby giving deference to William. The other half feared William, knowing he'd become lord of the manor when his father died. William's ego blinded him to both.

He walked to the bar and flipped a coin to the barkeep. It hit the counter with a tink, spun on end, and eventually came to rest on the surface. The establishment knew exactly what he drank. Each time he came in, one of the dashers quickly ran to served him a pint of the tavern's finest ale, a special brew kept in back for the more elite guests.

He took a few sips and scanned the room for his friends. Alessandra and Seth sat at a table near the corner, so tucked away that he hadn't noticed them when he first came in.

She was smiling and laughing, her hand touching Seth's arm frequently. The grin on William's lips fading as he watched.

Surely they saw me come through the door. Why hadn't they called out? What was so damned funny? Seth was never funny. Maybe he was making fun of someone—a pathetic attempt to win her favor.

Feelings of resentment and jealousy simmered within. He hadn't forgotten about their kiss in Mercel. But his distemper had faded on the journey back. Watching them flirt with each other tonight brought it all back.

He crossed the room with purpose, squeezing between tables. He saw red as Alessandra and Seth were giggling together like schoolchildren. In his anger, William accidentally bumped a large man seated at a table not far from Seth and Alessandra's. Some of William's ale sloshed out of his mug, spilling onto the man's shoulder and over his meal.

His dinner companion quickly tried to defuse the situation. "Easy, Tom. I'm sure it was an accident."

Tom was an imposing figure. A block cutter by trade, he was extremely strong and fit. Standing nearly seven feet tall and weighing three hundred pounds, he towered over everyone. His broad shoulders and big hands dwarfed the mug he was holding. His friends called him Big Tom. He sported a long, black beard with a touch of gray that matched his hair and thick brows.

He wasn't normally an ill-tempered man, but he was unstoppable when riled. Most people gave him a wide berth when he was in a foul mood. And the spilling of ale made him foul.

The music ceased when Big Tom stood. A pretty girl who'd been dancing froze in place. The crowd hushed. All waited with bated breath, unsure of what Tom would do.

A couple of the castle guards, who'd been having supper a few tables away, gripped their pistols. Two more guards at the bar placed their hands on the butts of their pistols. They all turned to face William and Big Tom, readying for a fight.

William's tiny body stood in the shadow of Big Tom. The sneer on the giant's lips didn't look good. Seth saw the guards, but after what had happened in the forest, neither he nor Alessandra knew whether the guards would help William or let Big Tom kill him.

Big Tom's chest was heaving when his companion broke the silence. "Sorry, Master William. Must have pulled the chair out a little when we sat down. I know that makes it hard to get past. Please, Sire, let me buy you another ale," the man said nervously, looking from William to Big Tom. "To make up for our putting that in your way."

Big Tom's eyes darted to his friend. He was not the type of man to back down, and nobody dared mess with his food. But he'd heard what his friend had said. More important, *whom* he'd said it to. Lord Parlimae's son.

Big Tom had seen the castle guards come and go all night. He knew some of them were still in the pub. He wondered if they would come to the young noble's aid. He knew William wasn't a problem, but could he take on all the guards?

William wasn't sure either. The guy was much bigger than him. But something had changed in William. A few days ago, he would have been afraid, nearly cowering. He would've been happy to squeeze out of a situation like this with his dignity. But he was not afraid now. With Big Tom's gaze turned to his dinner companion, William slyly grasped the handle of a small blade he had tucked under his coat.

Big Tom made the first move. "Sorry, Sire. Didn't mean to spill your ale." His deep voice rumbled between gritted teeth.

Apologizing was a wise move. The big man didn't know it, but William was prepared to gut him right there. This was not the same William who'd entered the Dark Forest. It was not the same boy reluctant to go into that alley in Mercel. He was still arrogant and spoiled, but now he was ruthless. Big Tom may have been bigger and more powerful, but he would have lost this fight. His friend had saved his life by mentioning William's title.

William relaxed the grip on his blade, though his eyebrows were still the vicious slashes of a man considering a kill. Seth saw the look on William's face and approached his friend cautiously. "Hey, we're over here," he said softly.

Without taking his eyes off William, Big Tom reached back and pushed the chair out of William's way. The force was so great that it jarred the table. Big Tom's friend raised his hand and shouted to the bar. "Another drink for the son of our beloved nobleman. In fact, a round for the house on me!"

That was all it took to break the tension. The crowd let out a giant cheer, and everyone raised their glasses and clapped. With the tension quelled, the music began to play again, and the pretty girl danced. The guards relaxed their grips on their pistols, retuning to what they were doing before the confrontation.

William nodded to Big Tom, then slid past as the giant sat down with his friend. A dasher came running over to fill their mugs with ale.

Seth was the only one brave enough to move during the tension. Standing by William now, he put his arm around his friend's shoulder as the two made their way to the table. "I thought he was going to drive you into the floor, my old friend."

The joke fell flat. William didn't like it one bit, and he stopped with an intense look. "What? You don't think I could have taken him?"

Seth pulled out William's chair. "No, no, I'm sure you could. I was just joking. He would have killed me for sure."

Seth sat, shooting Alessandra a quick look. Both felt William's ire.

"Why would he kill you?" William asked.

"You're my friend. I would have fought right there with you. I'm sure he would have killed me first," Seth answered.

William's expression softened. He smiled slightly and nodded. His anger began to subside as he remembered Seth was his loyal, longtime friend. One willing to sacrificing himself for William's sake.

Seth raised his mug. "C'mon. A toast. To William." He looked at his friend. "You saved our lives. We owe you our lives. I'm glad you're here."

Seth, Alessandra, and William clanked their glasses together and took big, slurping drinks.

"How was your father? Happy you completed your mission, I imagine," Alessandra said.

"You know my father doesn't always approve," William said, looking at Alessandra. "But yes, he was happy the supplies made it here."

"What happened in Mercel? You said you would tell us tonight," she said.

"Oh, not much, really. After you guys disappeared into the forest, I caught up with Captain Corsi and his other guard," William said.

Alessandra leaned in. "What was the special item?"

"I don't know. It was lost," William said.

"Lost? I thought it was in the livery. They were talking about it when we were in there," Seth said.

"It wasn't there. Somebody must have come and taken it. I think the highwaymen thought you had it. Probably why they were chasing you," William said.

"What happened between you and Corsi?" Alessandra asked.

"Not much. I hit him before he got out of the livery. He had little fight left. His guard gave up rather quickly too," William said.

"Lost the item and the coin box." Seth let out a low whistle. "I'll bet your dad isn't going to be too happy with him. I wonder if his loyalty will shift."

"Let's just say his loyalty is to me now." A small grin crept across William's face.

"Even though he intended to sell us? I think that is why they were chasing us," Alessandra said, still angry.

"You have nothing to worry about. I would never let that happen. Or would you prefer I kill him now?" William asked, his grin growing.

"No," she replied.

Raising his ale, William toasted, "To the Dark Forest. And all her secrets. She cannot defeat us."

Seth, Alessandra, and William clanked their cups together before taking big gulps. William raised his hand for another round. Alessandra grabbed their empty mugs and said, "I'll get them. I need to stretch my legs."

William watched her squeeze past the tables on the way to the bar. None of the men she brushed past gave so much as a glance. And none dared touch her. Normally, they grabbed any woman trying to squeeze by, but they all took notice of Alessandra's companion. It was not lost on William, and he beamed with pride.

"I think I'm in love with her," William said to Seth.

Seth's eyes got big. "Alessandra?"

"Yeah. I'm going to marry her someday." William watched her place the mugs on the bar, then turned to look directly at Seth. "Something wrong with that?"

"Not at all. Just never heard you say that before," Seth replied.

William's gaze landed on her again. "Sometimes I watch her when she takes morning rides in the forest."

"Really?" Seth asked, a little taken aback. "You mean as you are riding through the village?"

William realized what he'd just confessed to Seth. How it sounded. The booze was clearly loosening his lips. "It's nothing creepy," he said defensively. "Don't tell her either. It's just that when I'm out hunting sometimes, I see her. That's all."

Alessandra raised one of the empty mugs and waved at Seth and William as she waited for their refills.

Seth nodded. "I won't say anything. Does she know?"

"No, goddamn it. I told you not to say anything to her," William barked.

"No, of course not. I meant does she know how you feel?" Seth asked.

"You see how she looks at me? And the way she ran up and wrapped her arms around me when I returned with the wagons? You can't fake that." He paused, then said reflectively, "She must." A smile came over his face until Seth interrupted his thoughts.

"You sure about that?" Seth asked.

William looked at Seth with annoyance. "I know she kissed you in the livery. But you know that was my kiss . . . right? I mean, I was the one who took on the highwaymen in there. You just happened to cut her loose while I was busy dealing with Corsi."

He conveniently left out Seth's part in the rescue. But Seth knew it would not matter, at least not to William. It wasn't worth a fight—or William's wrath.

William regarded Seth with narrowed eyes. "Did Alessandra say something to you?"

"She hasn't said anything. Maybe you should tell her." Seth decided it might go better for their friendship if William made his feelings known to Alessandra himself. He would only resent Seth telling for him otherwise.

William's smile got a little bigger. "Maybe I will. Maybe I will, my old friend." He patted Seth on the back.

Alessandra returned to the table with three mugs heavy with ale. They hit the wood with a low thud. The froth from the ale splashed over. She glanced between them. "Will what?"

The boys looked at her with blank expressions. She rolled her eyes. "Maybe I will what?" she asked.

"Well, ah, maybe I'll, um . . . sleep in tomorrow," William stuttered. "Then I'll find me a worthy bride, but not tonight." He let out a hearty laugh. Alessandra laughed with him and raised her mug. Seth gave a nervous chuckle, raising his mug too.

The three of them ate food, drank more ale, and enjoyed the evening. The crowd began to thin as the night turned into early morning.

William was drunk by the time they decided to go home. Alessandra and Seth were also tipsy but not nearly as inebriated as William. When they stood to leave, William was having trouble walking. Alessandra motioned to a couple of the guards and asked them to help him get back to the castle. William fought their help, of course, staggering out of the tavern on his own.

The guards hurried after him, and Seth and Alessandra followed. Outside, William's pride finally gave way, and he allowed a guard to help him navigate his way to the castle. He bid his friends adieu with one arm over the guard's shoulder.

Seth and Alessandra waved their goodbyes as they started in the other direction. A crescent moon hovered in front of them as Seth walked her home.

"What were you guys talking about in there?" she asked.

Seth looked at her. "When? What do you mean?"

"When I went to get the second round, you guys looked pretty serious. I don't buy William's lame excuse. And you got very quiet after that. You weren't the same as you were before he showed up," she said.

Seth stopped. He thought about William secretly watching her when she took morning rides. William had tried to play it off as a coincidence, like he merely stumbled upon her when he was out, but he knew William was lying. He suspected William was spying on her when she was home—maybe peeking in her windows. But he couldn't prove it.

He thought about telling Alessandra what William had confessed. How he was in love with her and intended to make her his bride. The thought of William marrying her was too much. Seth may have been uncertain of her feelings for him, but he was sure she didn't love William.

He also didn't want her to overreact. They'd all had a lot to drink. It didn't seem like a good time to tell her. This could wait until he could think clearly.

As he stood there on the street, her big, brown eyes reflecting the stars as she waited for his answer, his mind shifted. The only thing he could think about was her.

He slowly and softly slid his hand up the side of her face, slid his fingers through her hair, and pulled her lips to his. He kissed her deeply and lovingly, their lips fitting together like two pieces of a puzzle. It was as if they were meant to be together. The kiss was long and slow, and a current of emotion flowed between them.

Seth's other hand settled on the small of her back and pulled her entire body close. Her hand moved up to his chest—not to stop the kiss but to feel his heart—while her other hand wrapped around his neck as she melted into the moment.

The kiss was everything she'd wished for as a little girl. She had fallen in love with Seth long before they went to Mercel, but as their lips locked on the empty street, she knew that for as long as she lived, she would never be as connected to another human as she was to Seth.

What she did not know was that the kiss also sealed their fate. William had turned just before he crossed the drawbridge. He watched as Seth pulled her close and saw the man he thought was his friend kissing his girl. And right after he told Seth how he felt about her. But he also saw something that he would never let go: Seth wasn't just kissing her; *she* was kissing him!

FIVE

NIGHTMARES
AND MYSTERIES

he violin continues to play. The woman's long fingers slowly move as the bow slides across the strings. A haunting sound permeates the village. An oversized moon hangs behind the large trees.

The buildings and homes are lifeless and nearly colorless. Except for the red doors. Not every home has one, but those that do provide splashes of color in a black-and-white village.

Alessandra watches the beautiful violinist as she moves forward, her bare feet soundlessly squishing through the mud. The bottom of her long dress drags across the muck, becoming soiled at the seams.

The buildings and homes stretch and contract as if moving with the music. Rich notes bringing them closer together. Other notes move them apart. As the music becomes clearer, the homes come into focus.

The trees in the background awaken. Fires rage in the forest, their yellow, orange, and red flames kissing the darkness. Ashes and embers float into the town as the woman continues to play the violin, her melody dark and brooding.

The song intensifies, and villagers show themselves. Nobody runs. There is no panic. They exit the houses and alleys, walking forward aimlessly. It's as if they have been lulled to sleep by the music.

Other expressionless faces stare out from the windows. Men, women, and children are mesmerized by the song, their eyes as black as the abyss.

Alessandra tries to scream. "GET OUT! RUN!" Nothing comes out of her mouth. The only sound is the song from the violinist. A feeling of dread creeps in. She can only watch.

Her eyes catch movement at the edge of town. Beyond the violinist, in the darkness up ahead, something stirs. In the middle of the street, a black figure shifts unnaturally. A sense of evil overwhelms her as she watches this . . . thing. Whatever it is, her instincts tell her it is evil.

The violinist never breaks stride, never stops playing, as she walks toward the evil creature. Her steps are slow and methodical, like the song she is playing.

The music becomes visible. Ribbons of notes meander through the streets, between homes, and down alleys, luring people from the homes, except from those with red doors. The music flows from her instrument in all directions, converging on the dark figure. The sound gets louder and louder as the violinist plays.

Alessandra's dread becomes terror. Those people are going to die. She knows it and tries to scream, but there is no sound. There is only the song. The first of the notes are about to reach their mark when . . . poof.

Alessandra sat straight up. Her face was covered in sweat, and her nightgown was soaked. Breathing heavily, she wiped tears from her eyes. Her breathing steadied as she blinked fully awake. It was just a dream.

Her mind raced to make sense of it. She tried to remember as much as she could, fearing she would forget the small, important details.

It wasn't the exact same dream she'd had when she fell asleep in the cemetery beside Seth. Yet it featured the same beautiful woman playing the violin. She couldn't understand how she knew the woman was beautiful. In neither dream had she seen the violinist's face. Perhaps she'd deduced as much from the rest of the woman's appearance: curly blonde hair cascading down her back; long, white, see-through dress; thin shoulder straps over a fair complexion.

The violin was worn, old, and well played. The music was haunting. And the song was the same in both dreams. Ever since the first dream, she'd been hearing the notes in her head.

She had recognized the village as the land where the abandoned church and forgotten cemetery now stood. She'd identified it easily in her dream despite the fire that raged against the darkness of the trees.

The biggest difference between the two dreams was the creature that stood or hovered at the end of town. What was that? Why hadn't the villagers been afraid of it? And why hadn't they feared the fire either?

She got out of bed, going to her window. A fresh pitcher of water and a basin sat on the table. Her grandmother added them to each room before retiring to bed every night. Alessandra bent down and splashed water onto her face. The dream still weighed heavy on her mind. *What does all of it mean?*

The sun was already up. Farmers were leading their flocks to the fields. The plow horses were already working near the edge of the forest. Though the workers were too far away for her to recognize from her window, she knew one was Seth.

A dreamy smile settled onto her face as she thought about the day before. She and Seth had left early in the morning, intending to be home by noon. But they ended up traveling all the way to the cemetery. Their passions got the better of them, and they didn't return until just before dark.

She didn't like going so far, but the abandoned cemetery was the only place they could be alone. The wolves had been cleared out by William and his guards, and Seth convinced her it would be safe. The poisonous flowers kept everything away, including the wolves.

It had been a year since they first stumbled on the cemetery, and the flowers had spread around the property's perimeter. They covered most of the block wall now, making the place even more secure. Nobody else knew it was there. And as Seth had said the first night they spent there, nobody looked for the living among the dead.

Before returning home yesterday, they'd agreed to talk to William about the cemetery. He had been on a hunting trip for the past couple of weeks, but she hoped he'd be back by now. A few days ago, she saw some of the guards that usually went with him. Maybe William had come home while she and Seth were in the Dark Forest. She decided to go to the castle and find out.

She put her hair into a ponytail, finished washing, and got dressed. Then she made her way downstairs. Her father had already left for the fields. William had gotten her mother a job working in the castle's kitchen, and it required her to leave before dawn.

The house was quiet, except for the sounds of her grandmother doing the day's chores. She felt bad about being late to rise. This was not normal for her. Usually, she woke early so she could help her grandmother. She enjoyed spending time with the old woman, even if that involved working.

But Alessandra wasn't feeling well this morning. Her stomach was queasy. And she was unduly tired, which seemed strange given her late start. She hadn't gone out last night, nor had she eaten much. Her mother was already sleeping by the time she got home. Her father came in the door right after she did, so he had no idea she had been out all day. She'd gone to bed early, tired from the day's ride, so why was she so tired now?

She heard singing as she came down the stairs, the sound getting louder as she approached. There was something familiar about the tune—a repeat of certain notes she had heard before. *Maybe one of the musicians' songs at the pub?* But she quickly realized it was the song from her dreams.

Her grandmother was at the hearth, frying some eggs. "Well hello, dear. I heard you getting up, so I started some breakfast for you." The moment her grandmother mentioned food, Alessandra's stomach rioted. She raced out the back door and to the corner of the house to vomit.

Her grandmother watched from the doorway with concern. Alessandra wiped her mouth on her sleeve, then she returned to the kitchen. Before she took more than two steps inside, her grandmother placed a hand on her forehead. Her brow wrinkled with concern. "You all right, dear? You don't have a fever."

"I'm OK, Grandmama." She took a cloth from her grandmother's hand to properly wipe her mouth. "Probably just something I ate."

"Picking dried meats at the Loudons' again?"

"They are so good, though," Alessandra replied with a smile. She didn't like lying to her grandmother, but the old woman would have been even more concerned if she knew Alessandra hadn't eaten lunch or supper yesterday, let alone the usual scraps from the smokehouse.

"Come, let's get you some breakfast. You'll feel better with something to eat." Her grandmother pulled out a chair for her.

"Grandmama, what was that song you were singing?" she asked as she sat at the kitchen table.

"What song, dear? What are you talking about?"

"The song you were humming when I came downstairs," Alessandra replied.

"Oh, that," her grandmother said. "It was just a lullaby my mother used to sing to me when I was a baby. Why?"

"It sounds familiar. But I don't remember you ever singing it to me. Or singing it at all," Alessandra replied.

"I don't know, dear. It just sort of . . . came into my head this morning. I always found the melody soothing. I hadn't really thought about it in a very long time," her grandmother said.

"What's it about? The lullaby."

"It has to do with the Dark Forest. A story about the fight between good and evil, wolves and witches. A bit scary, but it also reminds us that only love can defeat evil." Her grandmother gave her a questioning look before spooning eggs onto a plate.

"I must have heard that song in the village somewhere." She decided not to say anything about hearing it in her dreams.

Alessandra took a few small bites, but her stomach began to churn. She didn't feel like pushing it, so she finished the small bit she was willing to eat. Her grandmother didn't say anything, but her shrewd gaze noticed that Alessandra was not eating.

When her stomach threatened to empty itself again, Alessandra put the leftovers in a bucket. Nothing went to waste in this house. Scraps were for the neighbors' pigs. She took the bucket outside, dumping the slop in her neighbors' trough. The pigs came running with grunts and squeals. Her neighbors, who were tending to their backyard garden, waved their thanks.

Alessandra returned to the kitchen, setting the bucket just inside the doorway. "I'll be back later today, Grandmama. I'm heading to the castle."

Her grandmother kissed her forehead. "All right, dear. Have a good day." She watched as Alessandra made her way to the main street in the direction of the drawbridge. The majestic Castle Parlimae towered in the background.

The castle was a short walk from Alessandra's house, not much farther than the Three Fields Tavern. She crossed the bridge along with dozens of other villagers. Each morning, many of the townsfolk conducted business in the castle's courtyard.

The mighty drawbridge spanned a big ravine that shielded Castle Parlimae from intruders. Built on the edge of a mountain, with a waterfall to the west, the castle was well protected on all sides, and the bridge was the only means of entry.

A high stone wall, or bailey, encircled the grounds. Within this protective embrace, various buildings and shops saw to the operations of the castle. There were barracks and a livery, both used by Parlimae's guards, as well as a robust marketplace.

Some of the more exclusive shops were permitted to operate within the security of the bailey. Many of these served high-end clients who were willing to pay a premium for elaborate craftmanship. This was the place to find ornamental clothing woven from expensive linens by skilled seamstresses. And it was at the armory and blacksmith shops that well-to-do folks purchased exclusive, handcrafted armor and the finest weapons.

Some of the shops were well known throughout southern France, and many were run by villagers who didn't own a shop in town. The market provided a steady revenue stream for Lord Parlimae, who took a cut of everything.

Alessandra passed the butcher and smokehouse, both of which dealt in exotic meats. The goods were available to any who could afford them, but the businesses mostly supplied Lord Parlimae and his staff. Visitors were attracted to them as well.

While Alessandra's family didn't dine on such delicacies, her mother had encountered them through her work in the castle's primary kitchen. This kitchen prepared all of Lord Parlimae's meals, including feasts for his elaborate parties. It also provided food for the barracks. Her mother spent most of her time preparing meals for the guards. Occasionally, she helped prepare Lord Parlimae's meals, but only when the regular staff was unavailable.

Alessandra always enjoyed the activity at the castle. She liked to see the people shopping and enjoying themselves. The tink of the black-smith's hammer hitting the anvil rang throughout the grounds. The smell of fresh bread, pies, and other pastries escaped the bakery and provided a warm feeling. Even the potter's clay had a comforting smell.

But her favorite scent greeted her upon entering the castle. Lord Parlimae insisted on freshly cut flowers whenever they were available. They released such a pleasant aroma that even Seth, who rarely visited the castle, remarked on the way they smelled.

Most of the castle was open to all. Only the private quarters were off-limits. People came and went frequently during the day. The lord entertained formal requests of all kinds in his great hall. There was no throne, as he was not a king, but a seat of distinction loomed over a narrow table that stretched across the room. A row of chairs joined Lord Parlimae's seat on the far side of the table, allowing his court to join him as he addressed the people.

People brought their issues to him in this room. And often it was the location of an informal gathering, a place to share a cup of mead, wine, or another libation.

The chapel was next to the great hall, and many visited it on a regular basis. Some would stop to pray before seeing Lord Parlimae, while others needed to pray after. He often invited visiting clergy to give mass as a way to keep faith with the villagers.

Meals, on the other hand, were by invitation only and took place in the main dining hall. Lord Parlimae hosted dignitaries of all kinds in this room. It was the most ornate location in the castle.

Guards conducted their business in an office at the back of the foyer. This was near the dungeon's entrance. It was their job to keep the grounds secure, so they had access to all areas, though it was unusual to see them coming from any of the towers that anchored each corner of the castle. The structure were off-limits to common folk. Only the staff, Lord Parlimae, family, and guests were permitted entry. Two guards always stood at the base of each tower and rarely entered. Even they respected Lord Parlimae's and William's living quarters.

When Alessandra entered the castle, some guards rushed past her on their way outside. Given that they were always busying about the castle, it didn't seem unusual.

She was immediately greeted by Lord Parlimae. "Alessandra. What brings you here on this lovely morning?"

Alessandra bowed her head politely and smiled before speaking. "Is William here, my lord? I was hoping to see him."

"I'm sorry, my child. He is still away on his hunting trip. Hard to say when he will return," Lord Parlimae said warmly with a smile.

"He's been gone awhile now," she responded.

"Yes. I'm hoping he will return soon myself. Is there something I can help you with?" Lord Parlimae asked. She was tempted to bring up the events at the forgotten cemetery. He was always kind to her, and she felt she could trust him. But she and Seth had agreed to seek William's counsel first.

"I just haven't seen him in a while, and the three of us usually go on our first fishing outing this time of year," she replied.

"Three of us?"

Before she could respond, a guard came up from the dungeon. He walked over and whispered in Lord Parlimae's ear. The expression on Lord Parlimae's face changed from the jovial greeting he'd given her to a more serious look.

"If you'll excuse me, there is something I must attend to. The moment William returns, I am sure he will come find you." With that, Lord Parlimae turned and followed the guard. They disappeared down the stairs to the dungeon.

Alessandra was confused by Lord Parlimae's response. She'd recognized the guard who whispered in his ear. He was one of William's closest hunting mates. And she saw two of his other hunting companions going up the tower stairs. That was odd. William would not be hunting without them. *Was Lord Parlimae lying?*

But why would Lord Parlimae lie? He knew she and William were friends. Maybe William was still hunting, but that seemed unlikely. Yet who was she to question a lord?

Rather than leave, she decided to stick around a little while longer. She made her way to the kitchen through the dining hall. Lord Parlimae's crowning glory, the room was large and magnificent.

The heads of various animals hung on the walls, each a tribute to the hunting skills of the Parlimaes. William had become such a prolific hunter that his mounts filled nearly every inch of space.

She pushed through the door to the kitchen. The staff knew Alessandra well, meeting her first as William's friend and now as the newest cook's daughter. So when she walked into the kitchen, nobody questioned it. They just smiled politely and continued their work.

The space was as large and as opulent as the adjacent dining hall. A big square prep table filled the center of the room. Shelving lined the walls on either side. Every kind of spice one could imagine was within reach. More dried spices and plants hung all over the room.

An equal number of pots, pans, and cooking utensils filled every nook and corner.

At the back of the room was the largest cooking hearth in southern France. Cauldrons were boiling and pans were frying all hours of the day and night. The guards who had the night shift needed to be fed, and early morning breakfast required preparation, so the kitchen ran twenty-four hours a day.

Alessandra passed the entrance to an underground pantry, which held all the meats and vegetables. The coolness of the earth kept them fresh and always ready to eat. She made her way toward the back of the kitchen.

Her mother was at an oversize table next to the fireplace, kneading dough. Three other women were working beside her. Today, she was tasked with making bread and rolls for supper. The sacks of flour piled under the table, shelves of sugar before her, and other ingredients scattered about the kitchen would all be gone soon.

With her back to the dining hall, she didn't see Alessandra come in and startled at her greeting. She turned around with a big smile and gave her daughter a hug. "Hello, dear. What a pleasant surprise. What brings you here this morning? Is Grandmama OK?"

"Oh, yes. Everything's fine, Mama," Alessandra responded. The smell of the food in the kitchen was making her queasy again. She clutched her stomach and wavered slightly, which caused her mother to grab a nearby stool. "You alright, dear? Here, sit."

"Yes, I'm fine, Mama. Not feeling so well this morning. A bit tired."

"You want something to eat? I can get you something. Perhaps some bread to calm your belly," her mother offered.

"No, no. I'm fine. Not very hungry. Grandmama made me some eggs," she responded.

Her mother kissed her forehead, then grabbed a scoop of flour so she could continue working on the dough. Lucinda Moreau was not one to stop working, even when her daughter came to visit. "So, what brings you here?"

"I was hoping to catch William. Do you know if he is back yet?" she asked.

"Did you ask Lord Parlimae?"

"He said William isn't here. But I saw some of the guards William always hunts with," she replied.

"I'm sure the young master has many friends, my dear. I doubt the lord would try to hide his whereabouts."

Lucinda turned to a woman who was trimming and arranging flowers at a table near the side door. "Dru, have you seen William this morning? Was he at the breakfast service?"

The older woman shook her head. "Just Lord Parlimae. He had his usual breakfast at his usual time."

Dru picked up the vase of flowers and headed toward the dining hall. Before she got too far away, she added, "Best to concentrate on work and not the comings and goings of the lord and his son." She backed her way out of the kitchen, disappearing into the dining hall.

Lucinda looked back at her daughter with a funny expression, then said, "Sorry, dear. I don't think he's back yet."

"He's been gone a long time." Alessandra murmured to herself before returning her attention to her mother. "Mama, have you ever heard this melody?"

She hummed a few bars, quietly enough that only her mother could hear.

"Sounds familiar. Why?" her mother asked.

"I had a dream about a beautiful woman playing that song on a violin. Then I heard Grandmama humming it this morning," she responded.

Her mother looked at her with wide eyes, then scanned the room to see if anyone had heard. She reached over, pulling Alessandra gently by the arm, and drew her away from the others. "Keep that to yourself. Some people might misunderstand what you are saying," she said sternly.

"It was just a dream, Mama," Alessandra responded.

"I know, dear. But some folks might take your dream and your grandmother's song the wrong way. You don't want anyone labeling you as a seer."

"You mean a witch." Alessandra burst out laughing. "Mama, I'm not a witch. It was just a dream."

"I know that, but people have been burned alive for much less. Promise me. You speak of this to no one," her mother insisted.

Alessandra's smile faded. She gave a serious nod. Her mother's expression softened with relief, and she hugged her daughter tightly. "I'm sure you just dreamed about it because Grandmama had been singing. Keep it that way."

Before her mother could say anything else, the castle bells rang out furiously. The sound startled everyone. Alessandra rose from the stool, and everyone in the kitchen froze in place, staring at one another. After the brief pause, they hurried into action.

Most of them exited through the dining hall. Workers in the back went out the side door along with Lucinda and Alessandra. Everyone converged in the courtyard.

She spotted castle guards scrambling from the barracks, but her attention quickly shifted to a commotion at the main gate. Several guards on horseback had come through the village, making their way to the castle. The lead horseman held a long pole, which bore the castle's banner at the top. It was a signal of trouble and instructed the castle to raise the alarm.

A wagon followed the guards, its wheels clanking loudly as it rolled across the drawbridge. The procession came to a halt at the castle's steps. At the top of the steps, the large doors swung open. Lord Parlimae ran out, a group of castle guards at his side.

People rushed to the front of the castle to see what was going on. Alessandra did the same, pushing her way into the crowd.

Tension was turning to fear. As she neared, she spotted blood on the arriving guards' clothing. A couple of people in front were close enough to see the back of the wagon. Alessandra watched as they turned away, heaving.

The crowd buzzed with rumors of a woman's mutilated body and body parts from someone else. She overheard the guards telling Lord Parlimae that they had found them in the forest. There were no witnesses, and nobody knew the identities of the victims.

Lord Parlimae walked to the wagon. After looking inside, he turned his head and closed his eyes at the disturbing sight. Alessandra couldn't see the bodies, but *could* see the blood—enough of it that it dripped off the back of the wagon.

The physician came running from the courtyard and forced his way through the crowd. "Move aside! MOVE ASIDE! Let me through, damn it! Let me through," he yelled. His eyes narrowed when he finally saw the bodies.

"I want to know what killed these women," Lord Parlimae barked.

"You know damn well what killed them!" the doctor snapped.

Lord Parlimae's lips pursed. "Just see to them, Doctor. I'll be back to see you later."

He turned abruptly, storming back to the castle. Guards began ordering the crowd to return to their work. The frightened people moved away reluctantly. Alessandra followed the crowd, making her way back to her mother.

"I'd better get back inside, dear," Lucinda said.

"Aren't you worried, Mama?"

"I'm sure Lord Parlimae will see to it. He and his guards will protect us. C'mon, let's go inside." Lucinda may have been afraid, but she didn't show it to her daughter.

"You go ahead, Mama. I'm going back to town." Alessandra kissed her mother on the cheek, then turned to leave.

"All right, dear. Don't go too far today, OK?" her mother said.

Alessandra smiled sheepishly. "OK. I won't."

"I'll see you tonight, dear." Her mother watched her for a few moments before returning to the kitchen.

Seth had been in the fields when he saw the castle guards leading a wagon out of the forest. He'd stayed well behind them, riding Boggs back to town. When he got to the end of the village, he tied Boggs. A large crowd was coming from the castle, and he felt it would be easier to walk. He was almost to the drawbridge when he spotted Alessandra making her way across.

"What is it? What happened?" he asked.

"Two people were killed," she answered.

"What?" Seth's face was a mask of shock. "Who were they?"

"A woman for sure, but they couldn't find most of the other person. I couldn't hear all of it. The doctor took the bodies back for examination."

"Did you see William?" Seth asked.

"Lord Parlimae said he isn't back yet."

"Seems odd. When I was in town earlier, I saw some of the guards he usually hunts with," Seth stated.

"Maybe they didn't go with him."

"Maybe. But I don't think he's still on his trip." Seth looked up at the castle. He couldn't explain why their friend was avoiding them. And he really didn't understand why Lord Parlimae would keep William's return a secret. "You didn't tell Lord Parlimae about the cemetery, did you?"

"No. I told you I'd wait for William," she answered.

His thoughts became distracted when he caught her scent. Maybe it was the memory of their time at the cemetery playing with his senses, but he was almost sure he smelled the red door flowers in her hair. He moved a little closer, subtly touching her hand. "Will I see you tonight?"

Alessandra shyly looked in the direction of her house. Her father didn't dislike Seth, but he had other plans for her. Plans that were grander than his only daughter with a farm boy. He had no doubt Seth would be good to her, but he couldn't provide an easy life like William could. Yet despite the advantages of marrying William, she loved Seth. For now, she didn't want to tell her family.

The townsfolk who had rushed to the castle when the guards arrived were returning to the village. People went back to their routines with the utmost faith the guards would protect them. Everyone in the village believed Lord Parlimae had their best interests at heart. He had been good to them over the years.

She pulled back from Seth as another wave of villagers came across the drawbridge and walked past them. Not wanting to send the wrong message, she leaned in a little closer and whispered, "I want to see you too. I'll try to come to the pub after dinner."

She turned for home, but a few feet away, she spun back around. "Looks like it's going to be a full moon tonight," she yelled with a smile on her face and a spring in her step.

Seeing him always made her smile, even if it was only for a moment. A few seconds with Seth, and the uneasy feeling in her stomach had disappeared. The afternoon heat warmed her face, though her blush had more to do with a boy.

Alessandra believed nobody knew about them. This was mostly true. The villagers didn't care. None of them paid any attention to a peasant girl and a farm boy. What she didn't know was that William was in his room watching.

At the top of one of the castle's towers, in a bedroom overlooking the village, William watched the crowd disband after the wagon took the bodies to the doctor's quarters. He spotted Alessandra in the crowd, his gaze following her as she walked through the main gate and crossed the drawbridge. His desire for her intensified and turned to hatred the moment he saw Seth standing on the other side of the drawbridge.

He seethed when she stopped to speak with him. The crowd may not have noticed Seth touching her hand, but William did. His eyes turned red with rage. He couldn't hear what they were saying, but he could see them flirting. He hated her as much as he hated Seth.

From his perch high above, he followed her journey home. He lost sight of her when the main street curved through town. Buildings blocked his view, enraging him further.

While William stewed in anger, Alessandra bounced through the door to her home in good spirits. She found her grandmother in the kitchen.

"I'm glad you are back, dear," her grandmother said with a sigh of relief. "I didn't follow the crowd into town, but I saw the wagon roll by. What on earth is going on?"

"Two people were killed. Castle guards found them in the forest and brought them back," she replied.

"Oh my. At least you are safe. Best to stay in the village for a while."

"I always stay in the village," Alessandra said.

Her grandmother just smiled. She knew better, and was about to say so, when a strange look crossed Alessandra's face. "What is it, dear? What's wrong?"

After a few seconds of silence, she took Alessandra by the arm and sat her at the table. She sat across from her granddaughter, waiting patiently.

"Grandmama, about that lullaby you were humming this morning. I've heard it before. I've been having dreams about a beautiful woman playing the violin in a forest village. I think that is the song she is playing," Alessandra said.

"I see." Her grandmother raised an eyebrow. "Some believe dreams are windows to the unknown. Warnings. Signs. Even omens. But you've never spoken of such visions in the past."

"No, I've never experienced anything like this. And it's happened only a couple of times," she said. "Same dream—well, almost the same. It's the same woman going through this hidden village at night. Her song seems to hypnotize the people in the village, but I can't really see any of them. I can't tell if the woman is good or evil. But the dreams are dark, like a nightmare."

"Where is this village?" her grandmother asked.

"I'm not sure exactly. I think it might be somewhere in the Dark Forest," she responded. "Do you know what it means?"

"Dreams are often nothing more than the mind's restlessness. Pure imagination. You've always had an active one. When you were a little girl, you used to fight and play with the best of them, including those two boys," her grandmother said with a laugh. She patted Alessandra's hand. "I'm sure it's nothing."

"Mama says I shouldn't tell anyone. She's afraid I might get labeled a witch."

Her grandmother let out a hearty laugh. "Now *there's* one with a big imagination. Your mother, always the worrier." Her face slowly drained of humor. "But she's right. There are those who read dreams, like the singing and dancing folk who play in that pub you frequent."

"They read dreams?" Alessandra asked.

"Not all of them. But members of their community do."

"Then why aren't they labeled witches?"

"They are, dear," her grandmother said. "Haven't you ever noticed they aren't treated all that well? A few of them make a living interpreting things like dreams. And a dream like yours might get thought of as a dark omen."

"Are they dangerous? Those people, I mean."

"No more than anybody else. But they aren't overly scared of things they can't explain. Scared and paranoid people can be dangerous. Getting labeled a witch is nothing to joke about in our village—or in most places around the world." She walked over to Alessandra, giving her a big hug and a kiss to the forehead. "It's nothing to worry about, my dear. Best to keep it to yourself, though. Now, are you planning to see that boy tonight? The cute one with blond hair?"

Alessandra blushed. "I hope so."

"Then let's get your chores done early. Keep to the village for a while. Your dreams aren't nothing, but those murders are real. People will be panicked because of them." Her grandmother retrieved a teapot from the fireplace. She gave Alessandra a warm, comforting smile while pouring her a cup of tea. Alessandra took a small sip, drifting into her thoughts.

HUNGER OF THE WOLF

*T*he rest of the day was uneventful, both for Alessandra and the village. People went about their lives as usual. Farmers completed their work in the fields, then moved their livestock closer to the village, just in case the animal that had killed those people still roamed the forest. Fears had subsided, but the villagers weren't taking any chances.

Stores and shops closed a tad earlier. Owners wanted to have everything wrapped up as evening approached. The taverns in town took the opposite approach. They opened early to feed people but didn't close their doors before nightfall. Taverns were busiest after dark, and the proprietors all anticipated tonight would be even busier with the fear of wolves on the villagers' minds. People needed an outlet, and the gossip would flow when the wine and ale did.

Whispered rumors said the Dark Forest was haunted. Some called it cursed. The Beast of Gévaudan was mentioned in hushed tones at the Three Fields Tavern. "It ain't nuttin' like dat. Pack a hungry wolves is all. Superstitious nonsense. Damned forest always been dark. It's thick. Why dem thieves en highwaymen like it," said a half-drunken farmer who was chattering at one of the tables with some other patrons.

"That howling last night was strange," a woman said. "Seemed like it came from the castle. Then I heard it down the valley."

A man at her table scoffed. "I didn't hear nuttin'. I think it's yer imagination. All this talk about wolves and haunted forests."

Alessandra walked into the pub to meet Seth. The sun had set, and the moon was high in the clear night sky. The tavern was already full of anxious people. The hard work of the day had kept a lid on things, but leisure had blown the lid off. A few drinks brought out the villagers' true feelings.

Half the bar agreed with the drunken farmer. They concluded it was just wolves. Keeping their livestock close to town was being practical to prevent losses. Carrying muskets everywhere seemed prudent too. Everyone agreed the guards couldn't be with them every minute of the day, and nobody could afford not to work. The harvests weren't great lately, making every coin count.

The musicians took full advantage of the fear. They played a hearty song with an upbeat tempo to keep everyone's spirits high. Nobody knew it was a song of magic, wolves, and lost love. Their energy and enthusiasm kept the crowd's mood elevated, as did the girl gyrating to the beat. A buoyant crowd meant larger tips.

With the loud music and even louder crowd, Alessandra did not hear Seth walk up from behind. "You come here often, Miss?" he whispered in her ear.

Her face lit up, but he couldn't see it. She turned only slightly to respond. "You're late. Perhaps I should go. Apparently I'm not worth being on time for."

"I should walk you home, then. Haven't you heard? There are dangerous wolves all around," Seth responded quietly.

Alessandra turned completely around, a slight grin on her face. "So why are you late, kind sir?"

"I had to fight off a dragon just to see you."

She raised her eyebrow. "A dragon, huh? What kind of dragon?"

"A small one," Seth said.

"Well, dragons aren't real. Everyone knows that. Are you in the habit of lying to a lady?" she quipped.

Seth smiled. "Come on. Let's grab a table before there aren't any."

They moved to an empty table not far from the door. A dasher brought over two pints of ale. "You two are getting to be real regulars. Any supper?" Seth shook his head with a tight-lipped smile.

"So, why were you late?" she asked.

"Had to help my brother and sisters settle. The excitement today had them full of energy. After I saw you, I rode back to the fields. My dad had me take my brother to the house. My sisters were with my mom, but he didn't want us near the forest until this got sorted," Seth said. "You hear anything else? Your mother hear anything more from the castle?"

"Mama overheard guards talking about the bodies. They were found along the road, deep in the forest. Said it looked like they were being chased. Hunted."

"Are they from here? The two dead people? I haven't heard of anyone going missing. I wonder who they were," Seth said.

A man seated at a table next to them butted in. "I heard one of 'em was Jean Hobaret's wife."

"Who?" Seth asked.

"Jean-Pierre Hobaret. He runs Lord Parlimae's coaches and wagons. Nobody seen his wife in some time. Or 'im. Most figure 'im to be on a supply run to Port Calibre. Some round here think he may've killed 'er. Rumor says she was shaggin' somebody at da castle while he was on supply runs."

"What do you think?" Alessandra asked.

"Well, ya know, miss. Seems to me ain't nobody seen da young master in some time neither. Maybe he did it?"

A drunk man at his table leaned in. "Maybe da master was kilt. Might be de utter body."

"Shut yer piehole, ya drunk. If Lord Parlimae's son was kilt, he'd have da whole damn guard out lookin' for the creature who done it," the man said as he got up. "You be careful out there. These be strange times." The man grabbed his friend, dragging him to the bar.

Seth looked at Alessandra with some concern. "Wasn't that one of the women William was seen with at the castle? Madame Hobaret?"

"William wouldn't have an affair with a married woman. His father would never allow it," she responded.

"Are you serious?" Seth couldn't believe she was so naive.

"You haven't seen him, have you?"

Seth took a drink and shook his head. "No."

He didn't expect William to come and see him. If anything, William would go to her. Seth had never told her how William really felt about her. He'd kept the secret for a while now, and he just couldn't find the words to tell her about William's obsession. He found William's confession of stalking creepy, and he was sure she would too.

But he had decided against telling her back then and didn't want to scare her now, especially considering everything that had happened today. He would tell her after things calmed down, he decided. It was a conversation he was not looking forward to having with her.

He turned back to the issue of their missing friend. "Soldiers came through the fields this afternoon, sometime after they brought the bodies to the castle. They were patrolling and going into the forest, but William wasn't with them."

"Don't you think if he was back, he'd be with them? He wouldn't miss a chance to be in on that." Alessandra's eyes dropped to her drink. "What do you think killed those people?"

"If I had to guess, I'd say wolves. Maybe that pack returned, the one we saw last year when we first found the cemetery."

She looked around the pub at the people gathered. A palpable tension filled the air. She thought of her family. Her grandmother knew she was coming to see Seth, but her father did not. He might start wondering where she had gone and worry.

"It's getting late. I'd better get home," Alessandra said, drinking the last of her ale. Seth downed the rest of his and got up to walk her out. They were squeezing through some tables when the pretty dancing girl stepped in between them, blocking Seth's path. Alessandra laughed out loud at the look on his face.

He became visibly embarrassed as the girl grinded up against him. The crowd saw his face and erupted in laughter. A few of them yelled out to him as they slapped one another on the back.

The pretty girl licked her lips as she looked him over. It was all part of the act; she wanted some coin. He quickly dug through his pocket, desperate for her to let him pass. She winked at him and gave one last shimmy before moving on.

Seth straightened his shirt, gathered himself, and gave a weak smile as he walked out of the pub behind Alessandra. The crowd howled with laughter at his shy demeanor. The sound of the bar faded once the door closed behind him. Alessandra looked at him with a twinkle in her eye. "She was pretty. You liked her?"

"Of course. Who wouldn't?" Seth said playfully. He was still embarrassed but wasn't going to give her the satisfaction of a bumbling response. Alessandra just giggled. She wasn't the jealous and insecure type. Her love for him was pure. It was part of what made her so special.

Seth took her by the hand and led her into a darkened alley. The moment the darkness enveloped them, he pulled her close and kissed her lips firmly. The kiss was strong yet soft with a loving tenderness. She melted into him, wrapping her arms around his neck to get as close as she could. She wanted to feel everything about him in this moment.

As they kissed, he smelled the red door flowers in her hair. He loved the intoxicating scent. The aroma had hit him the moment he walked up behind her in the tavern, and he'd been imagining this kiss ever since. She tasted just as good. Their lips locked together like they were meant to be. This was a feeling he never wanted to end.

They gave in to their passions, confident they were hidden from view. Though they were only a few doors down from the tavern and a few blocks from her house, and though the full moon lit the street, shadows draped over alleys like this one. Nobody would see them, Seth thought. He didn't know William had been watching all along.

When the sun went down, William had snuck out of the castle. He crept through the village, keeping to the shadows as he made his way to Alessandra's house. When she left for town, he followed. He watched her go into the pub, then saw Seth walk in a few moments after. William tucked himself into a dark corner across the street and waited until they came out. He saw them sneak into the alley. Neither of them realized he was so close.

William wanted to kill them both right then and there. His eyes turned red with an anger he could barely contain. But he didn't stick around to see any more. His plans for them were more severe than a quick, albeit terrifying, death.

Neither Seth nor Alessandra saw William at the mouth of the alley. Though Seth's vision had adjusted to the lack of light, he only had eyes for Alessandra.

Seth pulled back, taking in her face. He couldn't help but stare. She was so beautiful. Her big, brown eyes captivated him. Her soft, reddish-brown hair cascaded down her shoulders. "I love you, Ally. I want to be with you forever. I don't want to hide anymore."

She reached up and touched the side of his face. She loved him too. On her busiest days, she thought of him. There was no one in the world she wanted to be with more.

When they were together, she felt safe. Loved. And he always knew exactly what to say, even in troubling moments. They fit together, and she would have no other.

"I want that too," she said. "I just have to find a way to tell my dad."

Seth said nothing. His gaze dropped to the street. She lifted his chin to look into his eyes. "He doesn't hate you. He just has other ideas for me right now."

"You mean William?" Seth said.

"He wants an easier life for me. He thinks living in that castle would be it," she responded.

"It *would* be an easier life than I can give you," Seth said.

And that was why she loved him so much. He wasn't trying to push her toward William; he just wanted what was best for her, regardless of what that would mean for him. She knew he loved her with the purest kind of love.

"I'm only happy when I'm with you. Nothing is going to change that," she said.

"We could run away together," Seth said, trying to make light of things.

"I can't leave my grandmother right now. She needs me. Be patient. We'll have our chance. Just know that I love you," Alessandra said.

Seth leaned in again, and their lips met. This kiss was soft but lasted longer than the last. Her heart was pounding like a steady drum. She could hear it and wondered if he could too. He pulled back slowly.

As their lips parted, all hell broke loose. At the far end of the village, a woman screamed. Alessandra and Seth snapped their heads to the east, where the sound had originated.

Villagers raced to their windows, but none ventured outside. Fear of the unknown prevented them from coming to the woman's rescue. They listened in horror to the sound of breaking bones and tearing flesh. When the night quieted, everyone knew she was dead.

Seconds later, Seth and Alessandra heard heavy footsteps running across the squishy ground. As the sound faded, a bloodcurdling howl filled the valley. Witnesses would later call it a wolf's howl, but the bravest would describe it in truer terms: It sounded like the cry of a werewolf.

In the easternmost part of the town, lit candles appeared in the windows and brought the homes to life. As the residents peered out over the street, a strange fog rolled across the ground.

Neither Seth nor Alessandra could have known what was happening near the edge of the village. A few blocks from the fields in an area where several barns rested was a place where true horrors were coming true.

Madame Darby Marcellus was a woman prone to give in to her primal needs. With her husband routinely visiting the pubs late at night, she was left alone with her vices. That night, he was at the underground tavern. He had drunk himself to sleep at the bar, as he often did.

While her husband was away, Darby had decided to play. She enjoyed ushering many a young man into manhood, and tonight was no exception. Unfortunately for her, the act of passion would be her last.

Long before Seth and Alessandra finished their first kiss, Darby was buttoning her blouse and leaving the barn where she had met her lover. As she stepped into the alley, she was attacked by an unknown assailant. She never saw it coming. A sharp claw raked across her back, the gashes so deep they nearly killed her on the spot. It happened fast and unexpectedly.

She released a cry for help that rang out through the town. It was full of pain, the scream of a dying woman.

A blow from a black werewolf knocked her to the ground. The beast stomped on her back with a giant foot, the impact stealing the wind from her lungs. As she lay bleeding and barely alive, the creature applied more pressure with its foot, allowing its claws to dig in. The force was so hard that it snapped her spine in two. Pop! Crack! The last noise from Darby Marcellus was the sound of blood bursting out her sides.

The young man she had just been with heard the commotion but didn't understand what he had heard. He was even more confused when he rushed into the alley. Moments ago, he'd experienced bliss like he had never felt before. A beautiful woman had done things that would've make his mother blush. Now he was watching a mythical beast crush the spine of a woman still bearing his scent. His gaze dropped to Darby's body. A look of fear had frozen on her face.

He could not move, immobilized by the horror in front of him. The monster looked over its shoulder, its glowing red eyes locking with his. Its long arms and clawed hands were splattered with blood.

The moon's light glistened off its black fur, and saliva dripped from its pearly white fangs.

Without a sound, the creature leaped at him. Before its paws touched the ground, it finished the transformation from half man to whole wolf. Now it was a sleek canine, and it covered the ground between them before the poor boy could move. As he was torn to shreds, his gaze fell on Darby's dead body, and his last memory was of their time together.

The black wolf opened its jaws wide, then clamped down on the young man's neck. The razor-sharp teeth pierced his skin, tearing through muscle and shattering his neck bones. He died within seconds, the same look of horror etched on his face. The creature held him in its mouth as his body went limp.

Two brave villagers, who'd heard the commotion from their nearby houses, came running down the street with their muskets ready to fire. As they rounded the corner, both men saw Darby Marcellus's mangled body lying on the ground beneath a thick cover of fog.

Beyond her, they saw a large black wolf holding a lifeless body in its jaws. Each of them recognized the young man.

The fog continued to roll in from the fields, but they knew exactly what they were seeing. Both rested their muskets against their shoulders and fired. "Shoot it! Shoot that son of a bitch!"

The flash of the hammer striking the flint blinded them in the darkness. When their vision returned a moment later, only the two dead bodies remained. The black wolf was gone. Their aim had been true, but their musket balls were useless against the supernatural.

Alessandra and Seth watched as people poured out of the tavern in a hurry. Even more came out of their homes. An angry mob of people carrying torches and muskets marched through town—toward the site of the attack, Seth guessed.

He wasted no time getting Alessandra to safety. He took her by the hand and ran the few blocks back to her house, careful to stay within the security of the crowd.

Alessandra's parents were standing at the door of her home. They had heard the screams and were now watching the townspeople stream through town. Their eyes widened at the sight of her. They were relieved to see she was OK, but her father wasn't happy when he saw Seth. "Come, get inside," he scolded.

Alessandra slid past her mother and father. Her grandmother waited inside the door and placed an arm around her shoulder, leading her to the window to watch the activity on the street.

Seth nodded to her father before merging back into the crowd. As the mob moved along, intermittent howls echoed throughout the village. The fog was so thick that it was impossible to tell where the howls were coming from. The cries seemed to come from all over, which convinced many villagers that it was the work of a wolf pack living in the forest. None of them realized it was a single werewolf.

The mob finally reached the bodies of Darby Marcellus and her lover. Women gasped and covered their mouths at the sight. Several grown men lost their suppers. As they all tried to make sense of the tragedy, a loud howl rang out from the Dark Forest. The gruesome sight and the heavy fog intensified the crowd's terror.

Seth elbowed his way through the thick crowd until he saw the dead bodies. The young man was about the same age as Seth's brother, and Seth had seen him around town. He recognized the woman as Darby Marcellus. He knew of her by reputation; she supposedly had an affinity for young men.

There were those in the crowd who called this the work of Providence. Both dead women had been promiscuous adulterers. Darby Marcellus had clearly been with this young man, and Madame Hobaret had entertained various suitors while her husband was away. It was God's judgment, the crowd said.

The gossips had no sympathy for the young man either. They said he wasn't a boy anymore and nearly a man and shouldn't have violated the sanctity of someone else's marriage. Some even suggested he'd had an affair with Madame Hobaret, though there was no evidence of such a thing.

Theories abounded, but no one could explain the body parts brought in with Madame Hobaret. That was ignored, perhaps because it was less scandalous. Or perhaps because it was more frightening.

While they waited for the castle guards to arrive, dozens of men with torches formed a barrier around the bodies. The moment the guards showed up, the howling stopped. The guards loaded the bodies into carts and took them to the doctor for examination. Everyone was ordered back to their homes.

The village became quiet. More guards marched across the drawbridge, moving into position along the perimeter of the town. Despite their around-the-clock watch, nobody slept that night. The entire village was on edge.

The fog faded when the sun rose. At first light, additional guards came from the castle to relieve the night watch. The calvary rode into the fields with muskets at the ready. Their mission: to hunt wolves, killing all they came across.

The village was upset about the bodies, and Lord Parlimae had not come out last night. By midmorning, the village atmosphere had calmed. As far as the townsfolk were concerned, there wasn't a madman on the loose, it was a pack of wolves—witnesses described seeing a black wolf looming over the bodies, and the howling pointed to an animal assailant—they trusted the guards would keep them safe.

The shops and stores in the village felt safe with the extra castle guards, but the farmers had to get back to the fields. Crops and livestock needed tending. The past couple of years had been harsh enough. Nobody could afford another bad harvest.

So it raised their ire when Lord Parlimae was not only absent the night of the attack but also the next morning. Four people had been killed, apparently by a wolf pack led by a large black wolf. Anyone missing was presumed dead, their bodies yet to be found. Had progress been made in hunting the beasts? Had they identified the dead?

The people needed answers and decided to confront Lord Parlimae. Before lunch, dozens of peasants went to the castle. An angry group filled the great hall.

Lord Parlimae listened intently. One villager after another came in to either give testimony or express concerns. Some made suggestions, and others made requests. It seemed everyone had an answer. Frustration and fear were evident; the townspeople wanted action.

Seth and his father made it to the great hall right after most of the villagers had arrived. Like their neighbors, they wanted to know if it was safe to work in the fields. The harvest was just beginning, and they needed to get started. The last thing anyone wanted right now was a delay.

"Everyone, stay calm. These two men have assured me they hit the black wolf," Lord Parlimae said, gesturing to the villagers who'd fired their muskets at the creature. Seth figured they'd raced to the castle at sunup to tell their tale to the lord. "It ran off, probably to die in the forest, as animals do."

"We heard howls long after those two fired their muskets—long after the wolf ran off. If they killed it, why were we still hearing the howls?" someone yelled from the back.

"Obviously you were hearing members of its pack. The animal that attacked our people has most likely been slain. My son has been tasked with leading men into the forest, tracking down the remaining wolves, and killing them. As you all know, he is an expert hunter. There is nothing to worry about," Lord Parlimae said.

"The young master is back?" a woman said from the crowd. "I ain't seen 'im in weeks."

"I'm here!" William shouted from well behind Lord Parlimae. He stepped out of the shadows. Seth was shocked to see him, and he wasn't the only one. He turned at the sound of a loud gasp and found Alessandra nearby. He whispered her name to catch her attention, and she pushed her way to his side.

"William," she said softly. "He's here."

"It would seem so," Seth said.

"Yet he didn't come to see either of us." Alessandra was a bit concerned.

"Apparently not," Seth said, refocusing on his friend.

"I'll find this . . . black wolf," William was saying. "If he's still alive. I am quite certain these two fine gentlemen have killed it."

The two men smiled. Only William and Lord Parlimae knew the smiles were forced. Lord Parlimae had, quite convincingly, arranged for them to tone down their testimony. He'd had them brought to the hall at dawn so he could explain what they needed to say for the good of the village.

"When I find the carcass, I'll bring home the head for all to see," William boasted. "Then I will hunt down every living wolf in the valley and bring you their pelts!"

"Does he look different to you?" Seth said quietly.

"Bigger," his father responded.

"More full of himself, I'd say. If that's possible." Alessandra rolled her eyes, then released a sigh. "I'd better get going. I need to see my mama before I get back. Papa didn't sleep much, and he was a bit grumpy this morning. He wants me home early until all this is resolved. I told him I was coming to the castle to see Mama. I need to go do that in case he asks. It is good to see you, sir," Alessandra said to Seth's father with a slight nod.

Seth turned to go with her, but she stopped him. "You stay here. I'll be OK. It's daytime, and there are plenty of people around."

Seth watched her leave. His father patted his back. "She's a great girl, Son. I'm happy for you."

"What do you mean?" Seth asked.

"It's OK. I know how you feel about her."

"That obvious?"

"I know you don't think anyone notices, but it's written all over your face—and hers. A love like that is rare and shines. The world needs more of it." His dad placed a kind hand on his shoulder. "We should probably get back to the fields. She'll be all right. The castle is safe."

"What about us?" Seth asked.

"I'm sure Lord Parlimae and the guards will keep us safe. They can't afford another bad harvest either."

Seth took one more look at Lord Parlimae and William. His dad gestured to the men. "You want to stay and say hello to your friend?"

Seth turned back. "No. I'll catch up with him later. We should go."

They exited the great hall with heavy hearts. Outside, the villagers buzzed with the same insensitive gossip they'd shared the night before. Despite the rhetoric, Seth and his father didn't agree with the religious zealots who claimed the victims had it coming. His father understood these were statements of fear, an attempt to give meaning to senseless tragedy. But Seth was young. To him, the crowd was callous.

As the townsfolk made their way back to the fields, Alessandra visited her mother in the kitchen. The ladies were happy to see her again and joked that she should take a job in the kitchen given how often she had been coming around.

But Alessandra was really waiting to catch William. Standing at the threshold of the open side door, she made small talk with her mother while watching the castle grounds. She was waiting for William to pass by on his way to the livery. She didn't have to wait long.

She ran across the courtyard as he was entering the stables. "William!" she called out.

He stopped at the door. "Alessandra. What can I do for you?" His voice and expression implied she was just another peasant, not someone with whom he had been close.

She was taken aback by his demeanor. Neither she nor Seth had seen him in some time. Despite her overt enthusiasm, he seemed . . . distant. "When did you get back?" she said gleefully as she caught her breath.

"A couple of weeks ago. I've been busy tending to some matters for my father," he responded.

"I wanted to talk to you. Well, Seth and I need to discuss something with you. We—"

"I'm sorry. I really need to get going. I'm afraid my father finds the murders of these two women worthy of my immediate attention."

"And the boy," she stated.

"What?"

"The young man from last night. The one who was found with Mrs. Marcellus," she said.

"Yes, of course. Not really a boy though, right? After all, he was shagging the old broad. And she was spoken for. If he was man enough to bed a woman like that, he was man enough to be killed for it," William said curtly.

"What do you mean *killed for it*? I thought a wild animal did that," she said, surprised by his harsh response. Her mind snagged on something else he'd said, but it took her a moment to find the right response. "She was married. Not just spoken for."

William gave a small chuckle as one of the guards arrived with his horse. "Yes, yes. Married. And of course it was a wild animal. That black wolf, in fact. I just meant it's a sin to commit adultery. I'm sorry, Alessandra, but I really must go. My father wants me to take care of this problem now. Can't have the peasantry delaying the harvest. Got to make sure people like Seth are kept safe."

Alessandra was surprised by his tone. "Seth is a farmer who helps keep us fed. And he's not just any farmer; he's your friend."

William mounted his horse, seemingly more upset at her defense of Seth. The rage inside him remained under wraps, but it festered. Several guards on horseback came thundering out of the livery, spurring William into action. "Really, Alessandra. I must be going. We'll catch up soon."

With that, he jabbed his heels into the sides of his horse. The animal sprang into a full gallop.

Alessandra watched as William rushed to the front of the group and led them across the drawbridge. They disappeared into the village, leaving a cloud of dust behind them.

As she walked back to town, she remembered her conversation with Seth yesterday. He'd known William was back, and he had suspected that Lord Parlimae had lied to her. That bothered her, as did William's behavior. There was something very different about him. Normally, he spoke to her in soft tones, but today he had been abrupt and almost annoyed.

During her walk home, she studied the people around her. They were afraid but optimistic with William leading the hunting party. Lord Parlimae had done his best to calm them with his words, but it was the stampede of guards that reassured them.

The people didn't exactly like William Parlimae, but they appreciated his sadistic side when it worked in their favor. Villagers had no doubt that he would kill all of the wolves, protecting the people from the animals' wrath.

Before doubt could take over the town, the peasants' fears were lifted. By evening's light, William and his men returned, drawing a crowd as they rode through town.

The peasants cheered when they saw wolf pelts dangling off the backs of the horses. The wolves William and his men had killed were much smaller, and none were the deep black of the wolf from last night, but the crowd didn't care. To them, the hunt was a triumph. The pack had been vanquished, and the pelts were more than enough proof.

Lord Parlimae greeted William at the bottom of the castle steps. Villagers streamed behind the procession of guards. A small crowd watched Lord Parlimae embrace his son. They were the picture of victory: a father beaming at the villagers with pride. Lord Parlimae raised his son's arm high in the air to a round of cheers and applause.

He kept his arm around William's as they went inside to the great hall. He called for a celebration and invited everyone to join.

Alessandra's mother was summoned to the kitchen to prepare a feast. In the meantime, servants carried barrels of mead and casks of wine and ale into the hall so the people could toast the hunters. The town had shed its unease, and the atmosphere was now festive and hopeful.

True, the black wolf was not among the many wolves William and his hunting party had killed. But everyone assumed the leader of the pack had retreated to the forest to die from his wounds. They would find him soon enough, the townspeople concluded. The threat was over.

But not everyone celebrated. The two men who'd shot the black wolf knew better. They were certain they had hit the black wolf and even more certain it didn't die. They didn't buy the story of it slinking off into the Dark Forest. If it had died, William and his group would have found the body. They suspected something more terrible was afoot.

The physician did not celebrate either. After examining the dead bodies and treating the guards' minor scrapes, he also knew better. But he was a servant of Lord Parlimae and would speak no more about it.

William and his father told everyone that the wolves were members of a rogue pack. The hunters would be making more trips to the Dark Forest within the next few days to kill any others. And if by some miracle the black one was still alive, William vowed to either kill the leader or drive it out.

The party lasted most of the day and into the night. People drank and ate, told stories, and enjoyed a respite from the horror. Many villagers left the castle before dark, returning to their homes. Despite the optimism, nobody ventured beyond the town borders.

Those not ready to go home filled the pubs. The taverns enjoyed more customers than usual. Seth and his father didn't attend the castle party or the revelry at the taverns. They worked longer hours in the fields to make up for lost time. When he finished helping his father, Seth assisted his mother with his little brother and two sisters.

With the kids settled, Seth's father turned in early. Now was his chance.

He sneaked out, chasing the nagging feeling inside him that urged him to make sure Alessandra was safe. He also wanted to ask her about William.

The darkness allowed Seth to creep through the streets. When he neared Alessandra's house, he moved even more carefully. She lived closer to the castle than he did. Her house wasn't far from Three Fields Tavern, and there was lots of activity tonight. He didn't want anyone to see him. He just wanted to talk with her briefly before she went to sleep.

He crept around to the back of her house, hoping to get a glimpse of her without attracting any attention. He would wait in the dark alley across the way until she came outside. It didn't take long for her to appear.

The back door opened, spilling light over the yard. Alessandra carried a bucket of slop for her neighbors' pigs. She dumped the bucket over the fence, and the food scraps landed in the trough with a plop. Excited grunts and squeals broke the quiet.

"Psst! Ally!" Seth whispered, just loud enough for her to hear.

She jumped back, clutching her chest. A brief, startled whimper escaped her lungs and caught the attention of her father. He came to the back door and yelled, "You alright?"

"I'm fine, Papa. The pigs startled me is all," Alessandra yelled back.

He looked at her skeptically, scanned the area, then said, "Come back inside when you're finished. I don't want you out late. Still might be them wolves about."

"I'll be right in, Papa," she yelled. She shuffled to the end of the fence so she could speak with Seth without anybody else hearing, especially her father. "What are you doing here? You scared the shit out of me."

"Sorry. I just wanted to make sure you were OK," Seth said.

"Yes. I've been home. We didn't attend the party at the castle," Alessandra said. Her father had watched William and the guards race out of town and then return to a hero's welcome after killing several wolves. Her mother talked of the triumph, but her dad wasn't convinced the black wolf was dead. And he wasn't about to let Alessandra leave—not until he was assured the threat of the wolf pack was over. When the sun went down, he preferred everyone stay safely inside.

"Did you speak to William?" Seth asked.

"Yes."

"Well, what did he say?"

"There is something off about him. He was different," she replied.

"What do you mean? Off how?" Seth said.

"I don't know. He was short with me. Angry, maybe. It was like he didn't have time for me. And you were right: Lord Parlimae lied. William has been home for a couple of weeks."

Seth hadn't planned to tell her about William's obsession, but hearing her describe how he acted with her made him change his mind. He was about to tell her everything when the back door opened again. He retreated into the darkness, careful not to let her father see him.

"Come on, Alessandra. You need to come in. It's getting late."

"Alright, Papa," Alessandra called. She turned back to Seth and whispered, "I'll find you tomorrow."

Seth watched her walk back inside. He stared at the closed door, his mind working out the puzzle that was the Parlimaes. The moment he saw William in the great hall, he knew Lord Parlimae had lied to Alessandra. What he didn't understand, was why. William had been home for weeks, yet Lord Parlimae had chosen to keep that not only from Alessandra but also from everyone in town.

William's reaction to her was strange too. He didn't sound like a man who, not long ago, professed his love for her. It certainly didn't sound like someone who wanted to marry her. *Maybe he lost interest. Maybe telling her doesn't matter anymore.*

SEVEN

A SECRET MUST
BE REVEALED

*T*he dream returned again. The moment Alessandra fell asleep, she was transported to the old village.

She recognizes it immediately: *the cemetery behind the church. The big stone wall surrounding the graves. The red flowers covering the iron gates and giving them the appearance of a solid red door. The gray vines dripping acidic poison and the vapor rising from the sizzling earth.*

She sees the surrounding hills against a background of dark trees. A bright moon shines overhead and illuminates the houses in town.

Alessandra has been to the abandoned church many times with Seth. In real life, it's the only structure that remains. The dream allows her to see the entire village as it once was. Rows of houses line a street that stretches to the base of a hill.

Faceless people walk through the village. Families hold hands, and neighbors tip their hats to one another, extending greetings as they pass. She strains to hear them speak, but the world is soundless.

Then the music begins. It builds slowly, barely audible at first but rising until she can hear the notes loudly and clearly. It is the same song as before, the haunting violin played by some . . . thing.

The beautiful woman with long, blonde hair walks toward her. The woman's face is out of focus, but the violin tucked under her chin is clear. Her fingers move across the strings while her other hand guides the bow. Her long, white dress blows in the breeze, the motion matching the haunting melody.

As the woman gets closer, her face starts coming into focus. A feeling of deep dread consumes Alessandra. Although she is desperate to see the face of the violin player, she cannot resist the pull of the darkness, so she turns around. In the distance, a figure emerges from the Dark Forest and walks toward her. His black eyes hold white flames that glow against his inky silhouette.

The violin player moves toward the dark figure, softly touching Alessandra's shoulder as she goes by. Alessandra wants to see her face— tries to see her face—but it's turned away.

The musician stops a few feet away, but her music is unending. Her bow glides effortlessly across the strings, and the melody eases the fear that had built up inside Alessandra.

The black figure continues his approach, the moonlight revealing clothes of a peasant and a hammer on his belt. His long, silver hair blows in the wind. His eyes are no longer black with white flames but a piercing blue. With his sharp, chiseled features, he is the most handsome man she has ever seen.

He stands motionless, listening to the beautiful music. A look of caring settles on his face. Alessandra's fear dissipates as she watches them stare at each other.

The man's head tilts to one side as the song takes an ominous turn. The mood shifts. His blue eyes darken, returning to black. Alessandra can feel the tension, and her overwhelming sense of dread returns.

The buildings begin to peel away. The town disappears. Only the abandoned church and cemetery remain. The red of the flowers covering the iron gates is once again the only color in a world of gray and black. The moon increases in size, brightening the Dark Forest.

The music stops as two large, clawed hands split apart the trees. Out of the shadows leaps an enormous werewolf. It emerges from the Dark Forest at a run, hurtling toward the man with a menacing snarl.

The beast is twice his size, with giant, razor-sharp teeth that glisten in the moonlight.

Alessandra is nearly overcome with emotion as the great beast leaps toward the man. The creature raises a mighty claw and rakes the man's face with a force so strong it sends him flying. He hits the ground, then rolls to a stop at the base of the church. The werewolf leans back, arms stretched to the sides, and lets out a ferocious howl. The triumphant roar shakes the trees.

The violinist stops playing. Blood and tissue from her love cover the ground. Alessandra cannot see her face, yet she knows the woman's mouth is open; she can no longer hear a sound, yet she knows the woman is screaming.

The werewolf turns to the violinist, a hungry look in its eyes. Alessandra grabs the woman's shoulder, pulling her back as the werewolf advances.

Its feet stomp the ground, sending vibrations down the street. Alessandra can see the deadly creature's face so clearly now. It is terrifying. She pulls and pulls on the woman, but the violin player is defiant. She screams at the beast, unafraid as she points the bow of her violin at it.

Then she sees why the woman refuses to flee. The cemetery gates are open, and a child runs toward them. The werewolf looks over its shoulder at the child. A devious smile crosses its face. Alessandra knows the child is about to be killed.

And then the child is gone. Alessandra may not have seen it happen, but she knows the beast killed the child. Sorrow and terror fill her thoughts.

The music returns, drawing Alessandra's attention back to the street. The violinist is behind the werewolf, playing the haunting song. Somehow, the man has returned, though she can't fathom how he's still alive. He stands in the street, squaring off with the creature.

Fog rolls in, covering the ground and consuming the forest. The dream starts shifting faster now.

Alessandra blinks, and the forest village returns.

She blinks, and she is once again in the center of the main street.

She blinks, and the violin player now stands behind the man and the werewolf. The woman moves the bow across the strings, sending a tempest of music into the night. No matter how hard Alessandra concentrates, she cannot see the face of the woman standing right across from her.

A loud roar draws her attention to the werewolf. The man pushes a large spear through the great beast. The wide point bursts through the back of the beast and splits the creature's spine.

Alessandra studies the man, who appears at once similar and entirely different. His clothes are black, no longer the peasant garments he wore earlier. A ruffled white shirt with fancy cuffs peeks out from under a long, black coat. His knee-high boots dig into the dirt, giving him leverage as he shoves the spear deeper into the beast.

His skin is pale white, maybe gray. And his long, silver hair is swept to one side. Three deep scars run down the side of his head and across his face. White-flamed eyes shine above lips pulled into a devious grin. Alessandra can tell he enjoys watching the werewolf die.

That was the single image she remembered when she awoke. As with most dreams, most of the details escaped her. There was the song. The red door flowers. And the satisfied smile of the man who killed the werewolf.

As time went on, her mind would not be able to distinguish between memories and dreams. For now, though, the line between the two was crisp and clear.

It was the middle of the night when she awoke from the nightmare. She had turned in early after seeing Seth in the alley. After her father had questioned who she was speaking to out there (why, the pigs, of course), she thought it best to retire early and avoid further questions.

The nightmare had been disturbing. For a moment, there was love, but the dream turned dark quickly. She never did see the violinist's face, but the song was in her mind.

Who were the people in her dreams? Was this some kind of omen? And why was there a werewolf? The mythical creature was the only thing stopping her from believing the dream was some type of a sign. But still, it could hold some meaning.

She needed answers. Maybe the Travellers would be at the pub. Her grandmother had said they interpreted such things.

She peered out her bedroom window. The moon and stars looked peaceful. She had no idea what time it was, but the moon was high enough in the sky that the pub would still be open.

She got out of bed quietly and put on her clothes. The door creaked slightly as it opened. Her father's snoring was loud enough to hear from the hall. As long as he was snoring, she could get outside unnoticed.

Her feet made no sound as she tiptoed down the stairs and across the house. She closed the front door behind her and stepped out into the night. The temperature had dropped, and the air was cool. She wrapped a shawl around her shoulders as she walked up the street. As she passed a rain barrel on a neighbor's lawn, she saw her reflection in the water. The moon's light brought out the red of her shawl. Alessandra wasn't a vain young woman, but she vowed to buy a cape if she ever had enough money.

Three Fields Tavern had not yet closed for the night, but there wasn't any music, and the crowd was subdued. Alessandra removed her shawl and glanced around the place. It seemed most people had gone home early, and the few customers who remained paid her no mind. They chattered about the wolves and William and whether danger still lurked in the area.

The two men who had shot the creature went along with Lord Parlimae's plan to keep everyone calm. They maintained the lie—until they had a few drinks. And while many of the peasants ignored them, choosing to believe the less frightening version and trusting that William was more vicious than the black wolf, others were becoming suspicious.

Alessandra moved passed a table of men debating the issue and searched for the Travellers. To her disappointment, they were not there. "The musicians with the girl," she said to the bartender, "where are they?"

"They took the night off, young miss. Back at their wagons, I suppose."

A semidrunken patron at the bar spoke up. "If they are still around. Taken off altogether if they be smart."

"What do you mean?" Alessandra asked.

"You don't actually believe that the lord's bumbling son managed to kill the beast that murdered our neighbors, do you?" he said.

"He's gotten a lot bigger since he returned from his hunting trip. And he always was a devious little bastard. Cruel, some might say. I think we can all assume he got them. People need to get back to the business at hand and forget all this nonsense," the bartender said.

"Do you know where their wagons might be?" Alessandra asked.

"They were camped at the eastern edge of town. There is a small patch of open ground inside a chestnut grove. You might find them there. They may be gone, as he said. Best not to go out there tonight, Miss. They'll be there in the morn if they be still around," the bartender replied.

Alessandra thanked them and left the pub. She pulled her shawl back over her head as she walked down the main street and toward the drawbridge. Instead of crossing the bridge to the castle, she turned and made her way across town. The large torches on the castle walls provided light for her journey and illuminated the castle.

The low hum of the waterfall to the west made the walk calm. During the day, the hubbub of the village drowned out the soothing sound. At night, under the stars, the deep tones echoed the closer you walked to the ravine.

It didn't take long for her to reach the far end of town. The chestnut grove was less than a quarter mile past the last building. It was dark, but she could see a faint glow coming from behind the trees. The Travellers must have still been in town, and the light must have been their campfire.

She approached cautiously, calling out softly as she pushed through the trees. It wasn't polite to enter someone's camp without announcing yourself.

Three wagons were in a semicircle within the tiny space. The grass was trampled down between them, and a small fire sat in the center. The Travellers had lined the firepit with rocks to prevent it from spreading to the grass.

Four people stood as she came through the trees. She recognized the two musicians and the pretty girl who'd teased Seth the other night. There was an unfamiliar older man sitting around the fire. He had not gone to the pub with them. He wore a short hat with a loose-fitting blue shirt and was clearly the elder of the group.

Alessandra scanned the camp, not surprised to find it packed and ready to go. No doubt the four of them had split with their caravan to earn money for their community in the village of Parlimae. With winter approaching, they would be getting ready to leave the village and meet with the rest of their group. It seemed the murders in town had expedited their departure. The camp was so empty that Alessandra wouldn't be surprised if they planned to leave at first light.

Alessandra stepped into their circle. "Bonjour," she said sweetly.

The pretty girl was the first to respond. "Bonjour. What is it you want? A bit late to be out for you, no?" She took a few steps toward Alessandra.

"I am sorry to intrude. I was told you know how to interpret things," Alessandra said.

"So all Travellers are magical, then? You think we're all alike?" the girl said. One of the men chuckled. "Or maybe you are here to say I'm a witch. Revenge for dancing with your man."

"Oh, no. Of course not. I mean no disrespect, sir," Alessandra said to the older man, then turned to the pretty girl. "And he loved it. Anyone would. You're beautiful." She paused to take a deep breath before explaining. "It's just, well, I've been having these dreams. . ."

"Dreams? You mean you've come to the edge of town with a killer roaming about to tell us about a silly girl's dreams? Bit of an ego on you, I'm afraid," the pretty girl quipped, then addressed her companions. "Don't you think?"

The younger men chuckled as the elder cleared his throat in disapproval.

"Arrabella, stop teasing her. Go on, girl. What kind of dreams?" The elder sat back down, extending his hand in invitation. Alessandra sat on an empty stump. "Pay no mind to Arrabella. She is just tormenting you. She finds it amusing."

The pretty girl giggled. Her stern expression disappeared, replaced by a devious smile. She handed a cup to Alessandra, who took it with a skeptical look on her face. "It's just tea, love. But I can add something stronger, if you like."

Alessandra smiled. "No. No, thank you." She took a sip, then turned to the elder. "I keep having these nightmares and don't know what they mean."

"Why do you assume they mean anything?" he asked.

"I don't. But they weigh on my thoughts. I need to know if they mean something."

The old man stood as he spoke. "When was the last time you had one of these dreams?"

"Papa, no!" Arrabella pleaded.

"Shush!" he responded sternly.

"I woke from one just a few hours ago," Alessandra replied.

"Come, child. Let us find out if there is any meaning to what plagues your mind." He strode in the direction of his wagon and motioned for her to follow. The two men remained outside, but Arrabella joined her father and Alessandra.

The girl held a stick to the fire until it ignited, then she used it to light several candles and a lamp inside the wagon. Her father removed his hat and hung it on a deer antler mounted on the wall. The wagon was filled with many things: various trophies and knickknacks of all kinds, strange dolls, small toys, paintings, and other forms of art. But what caught Alessandra's eyes were the mystical objects and strange symbols. She spotted astrological signs, star maps, depictions of strange beasts, and other unworldly things.

A curtain hung in the middle of the wagon. A small table sat off to the side, surrounded by several chairs. The elder dragged it to the center of the room and then retrieved three chairs. While he arranged the furniture, Arrabella disappeared behind the curtain.

Alessandra sat across from the elder. A moment later, Arrabella returned. She covered the table in a red cloth, then carefully placed a deck of cards in the center.

"Cards?" Alessandra said.

"Don't be disrespectful, girl!" Arrabella snapped. "These are not ordinary cards. Someone skilled in reading can see the future or unlock mysteries of the past."

"You can tell me about my dreams from them?" Alessandra asked.

Arrabella laughed. "Not me, foolish girl."

The old man looked at Alessandra with a serious expression. "You must tell us about your dreams so we may know what to ask the cards. If asked correctly, they can tap into the knowledge of the universe."

"Well, I—"

"Not yet, child." The elder picked up the deck and began to shuffle the cards. "I am going to hand these to you. Shuffle the cards like this while you tell us about your dreams. You must concentrate on the dreams the entire time you handle the cards. Do not think of anything except the dreams. Tell us everything you can remember. Leave nothing out."

The elder finished shuffling the deck and handed it to Alessandra. She moved the cards in the manner he'd demonstrated. As they flipped through her hands, she recounted the three dreams.

She did as he asked but left out one tiny detail. She told them of the old church, the cemetery, and the red flowers covering the gate, but she left out the location. The abandoned church and cemetery were a refuge for her and Seth. It was their secret space, and she didn't see the point of revealing where it was.

When she finished describing the dreams, she set the deck down in the center of the table.

"Now split them in three piles," the elder Traveller instructed. Alessandra hesitated, so he said, "Don't think about it. Just do it."

Alessandra did as he asked and placed the piles in front of him. He nodded in approval. "Now put them back together in any order. As you do, concentrate on the questions to which you seek answers."

Again Alessandra did as he instructed, combining the piles into one deck. She placed it directly in front of him.

The elder slid the deck to one side, clearing the middle of the table. Then he pulled the deck toward him and spread the cards. One slid out of place, jutting toward the middle of the table. The movement was slight, but it was clear the card was no longer in line with the deck.

He pulled the card from the pile and slowly turned it over. It depicted a crescent-shaped moon hanging in a starlit sky. A long tear was dropping from the corner of the moon's eye. A crab held on to the bottom of the moon. Each end of the crescent appeared to be melting to the ground.

"The moon allows you to see in the night. The sky is bright when the moon is out. You can see the stars. Your dream was equally as revealing. You could see everything that was happening. In your dreams, the moon is always overly big and bright, illuminating the village and allowing you to see. This card suggests there is a secret before you that has yet to be revealed."

"A secret?" Alessandra said with apprehension. Her heart skipped a beat. Her voice wavered with a small amount of fear. Her thoughts raced. There was what happened in Mercel. There was the forgotten cemetery. And there was the red door. But something inside her knew: The card was pointing to something else. A voice inside her said it was a secret she needed to tell Seth.

"Yes, child, a secret. Is there something you are keeping from someone? Something you need to share?" The elder looked closer at the card. "There is more—a tear falling from the moon's eye."

"Does that mean sadness?" she asked.

"Not necessarily. Remember, you are asking the cards about your dreams. They deal with much darkness, not just in the sense of night. There is a dark, evil creature. But there is also love, two people finding their way to each other. The song guides them."

"You can't mean me," she said. "I don't play an instrument."

"You are not the violinist. I believe the two people in your dreams are a reflection of the past. The dream allows you to see them. They are trying to find each other, but evil surrounds them. Right before the final fight between the werewolf and the man, you felt their love. Love is joy. The tear may represent joy."

Alessandra tapped the card. "The moon is melting. What does that mean?"

"It indicates nothing is forever, not even the heavens. It drips down, signifying something is pulling at you—like the crab pulls at the moon. Its claws won't let go. Perhaps this has to do with that secret you need to tell. The two people you see in your dream may be telling you to unburden yourself before it is too late. We must go again," he said, collecting the cards and handing the deck to her. "Shuffle these once more, then place them in three separate piles, just as before."

Alessandra did as he asked. Again he fanned the cards; again one slid out of line. He placed the card faceup on the table. The death card. Alessandra took in a noticeable breath. He glanced at his daughter quickly before looking back to Alessandra. He slowly placed the death card next to the moon card.

"Does this mean I'm going to die?" she asked.

"No. The death card does not always mean death for the subject of the reading. Let us not forget to take it in context of your dreams. You charged the cards with deciphering your dreams when you shuffled them and concentrated on your dreams."

"In your final dream, the werewolf attacked but did not kill the man. You believe it killed the child, although you did not see the death. Then the man killed the creature with a spear. We are in the time of muskets. Few use spears as weapons anymore. I believe you are witnessing a past. Was there anything special about the spear?" he asked.

"I don't know. It was plain. The blade looked . . . old?"

"What spear is capable of killing a werewolf?" he asked.

Alessandra sat back in her chair. "Werewolves aren't real."

"Aren't they?" His voice held a challenge.

Alessandra looked up at Arrabella, who raised an eyebrow. Her expression suggested werewolves *were* real and that she couldn't believe Alessandra didn't know it.

"Do you really think an ordinary wolf killed the people in your village?" Without waiting for a response, the old man continued. "Wolves consume their prey. They don't drag it into the woods and leave it for the buzzards and worms. And there are much easier things to kill than humans. There are dozens of animal herds around this town. And the largest barns are on the end of the village, where easy prey sleeps."

"Madame Marcellus and the young man were found near a barn," Alessandra said.

"A horse barn. You believe wolves would go past cattle or even easier prey, such as goats, sheep, and the many chickens in this place?"

She had no response—his argument made too much sense. The man held her gaze. "Your dream is telling you of the evil that plagues this village. The Dark Forest surrounds Parlimae just as it surrounds the village in your dreams. It will hide the bringer of death until the creature no longer needs to stay hidden. It is in your dream as it is here."

"So I should stay out of the Dark Forest?" she asked.

"We should all stay out of the Dark Forest, my dear. But I fear the village of Parlimae is even less safe. I think that is what the card is telling us about your dream. The danger in your dream occurs in the village," he said. "But there is something else with this card. Do you see what's in the corner? A flower. You said the cemetery in your dream had red flowers that covered the gates. I think the flowers have something to do with death. After all, they are in front of the cemetery. It's as if they shield against death. Does that mean anything to you?"

She shook her head. She didn't mention that the same flowers guarded the same cemetery in the very real Dark Forest—or that they had protected her and Seth. They had shielded against death back then, but they strangled the village in her dreams. Good or bad, they were certainly a symbol of death.

"I'm afraid we must go again," he said.

Alessandra picked up the deck, leaving the death card and moon card on the table. She shuffled, split the deck into three piles, and stacked the cards in a single deck, which she set down again.

The elder fanned out the cards. This time, none of them moved out of line. He inspected the cards closely but could not find any that stood out.

"Now what?" Alessandra asked. She had watched his selection of the first two and realized he picked the cards that jumped out of alignment.

"Close your eyes and place your finger on one card. Concentrate on your dreams," he instructed.

Her finger landed on a card far to the right. It wasn't the last card, but it was close. The elder pulled the card from under her finger. She opened her eyes to find him scooping the remaining cards into a pile and setting them aside.

He set the card facedown next to the other two. She looked at him with anticipation, but he didn't immediately flip it over. "Concentrate on your dreams, on a question you have," he said. "Then turn over the last card."

Alessandra glanced from him to Arrabella. She lifted the corner of the card, then quickly flipped it over. The card featured a scale of justice against a sky full of stars.

"Justice is generally a good card. It sits next to the death card in this reading. The werewolf kills the child, but the man achieves justice when he kills the beast in your dream. Looking at the spread before us, I believe your dreams are telling you two things: You must reveal your secret. The fear of death should not dissuade you, as there is justice for you. The moon lights your path. It cries for you to do what is right, even as the burdens of this world pull you down."

"What about the song?" she asked.

"Music is a guide. It has been leading you to this place," he said.

Alessandra sat back for a moment. Her eyes looked over the cards and her mind replayed his words. Everything he said fit together. She had gotten answers, but she was plagued by more questions. But the elder Traveller would have no more of it. The reading was over, and the cards had spoken.

She wondered what the church would say about the reading. Her grandmother's words whispered softly in her mind, as did her mother's. Would the church brand her a witch? Alessandra wasn't sure she believed the cards' message, but a nagging thought said nobody could have known she was hiding a secret. And there was only one person the cards could be pointing to: Seth.

She stepped out of the wagon gingerly, then hurried away from the camp. She had lost track of time during the reading and couldn't dally.

Arrabella and her father watched as Alessandra walked out of the chestnut grove.

"You think she will tell anyone?" Arrabella said. Before her father could respond, she added, "Maybe we should have told her we knew."

"I am not sure that would have helped her. Sometimes a nudge is better than a shove, my dear. You of all people should know that," he said. "Besides, I may not be *drabarni*, but I don't think Rosalita would have minded our helping a young woman find her way."

"Maybe now she will understand werewolves are nothing to joke about," Arrabella said.

"Pack up, Daughter. We're leaving before things get worse around here."

The two Travellers tending the campfire poured water over the flames. Arrabella and her father packed up the remaining items to get the wagons ready as Alessandra walked along.

Alessandra walked out of the chestnut grove, leaving the camp behind, and she didn't look back. She had a lot to think about as she walked along. The castle torches and the warm hum of the waterfall kept her company as she made it back into town. She wasn't convinced those cards meant anything. None of her family believed in super-stitious nonsense. It was doubtful the church would approve. Father Gregoire would advise her to pray. And the idea that werewolves were real was beyond what she could accept.

She made it home to find her father still snoring. It was easy to sneak back up the stairs without waking anyone. *He might have gotten louder.*

Alessandra fell asleep right away, despite fearing she'd fall into another nightmare. A rooster's loud call woke her early. The late night left her exhausted, but she forced herself to get up. She didn't want to miss helping her grandmother with the morning chores again.

She splashed water on her face, then paused to watch the sunrise through her window. She got dressed and went downstairs quickly, expecting to be the first one up. But her grandmother had beat her to it. The smell of breakfast quickly hit her nose, and just as quickly, she became sick.

She didn't even say good morning, as she ran through the kitchen and out the back door to vomit. This time, she didn't make it to the corner of the house. Her grandmother followed her out with a bucket of water.

"It's OK, dear," her grandmother said as she poured the water over the vomit to wash away the smell.

Alessandra went back inside, but the smell was overpowering, and she raced back outside again. This time, it was just dry heaves. She sat on a small bench behind the house, holding her stomach. The nausea would pass if she didn't smell any food.

Her grandmother sat down beside her. She placed a tender hand on Alessandra's arm. "Is it the farm boy's?"

Alessandra's eyes widened. "How do you know?"

"I'm your grandmother, dear. You think I don't know my own granddaughter? Did you see him last night?"

"You knew I was out?" She was surprised, although she should not have been.

Her grandmother laughed. "It's a little hard to hear things with your father's snoring. Sounds like wild boars running all through the house. But yes, I heard you go out and come back. It's the bane of old age, dear. You don't sleep much. So, did you go see him?"

"No. I went to see those people you told me about," Alessandra said.

"About your dreams?" her grandmother asked.

"Yes."

"What did they tell you?"

"They said I have a secret I need to share." Alessandra paused, then added, "Looks like they were right."

"Not with me, dear. With him," her grandmother said.

Alessandra looked at her with tear-filled eyes. "But Grandmama, what if. . ."

"He loves you, Alessandra. He's a good boy, strong and loyal. But most important, he loves you. You must tell him. A child needs its father," her grandmother said.

"What about my father? Papa will be so disappointed." She was nearly crying.

Her grandmother pulled her close, hugging her tightly. "Your mother and father love you. They will always love you. And they will love their grandchild as I love you."

"But Papa has plans. He was hoping William would marry me."

"Your father only wants a better life for you. He doesn't see William for who he really is. And he will love Seth. Believe me." She pulled back to wipe the tears from Alessandra's face. "Take the mare. I already saddled her. She needs a stretch, and you need to see your man. Trust in the love you have for each other. Love is the only thing that matters, dear."

Alessandra regarded her grandmother with loving eyes. This dear, sweet woman was right. The cards had also been right. She needed to unburden herself and share the secret with Seth. She knew that he loved her and that they would be together forever.

Her grandmother walked with her to the back of the yard. The old mare was tied to the fence, saddled and ready to go. Alessandra climbed into the saddle and looked out over the fields. The farmers were already out there, tending crops.

"Thank you, Grandmama," she said, returning her grandmother's warm smile. She turned the horse around and trotted down the alley. After she reached the end of the town, she snapped the reins, encouraging the old mare to go faster.

The sun was shining brightly as the horse galloped along the main path through the fields. Seth would be near the Dark Forest, farthest from town. She pictured him hearing the news, elated she was carrying his child. She imagined him holding her and their deep embrace. How his lips would taste as they kissed joyfully. She envisioned their marriage in the chapel of the castle, Lord Parlimae officiating. William would be the best man and her grandmother the maid of honor.

Yes, the sun was shining brightly that day. The wind was blowing through the fields and over the crops. Amber waves of gold awaited the harvest. And the love of her life stood just beyond the last knoll in the road. Today would be the beginning of their story.

A smile stretched across her face. The excitement of seeing him and sharing their joy made her giddy. Their child had been conceived in the most unlikely place, with flowers protecting it against evil. It was a sign. Even the dead feared the poison from those thorns. What a story this would make. It held a special place in her heart, behind the flowers Seth called the red door.

THANK YOU

Thank you for reading *Red Door*. If you already purchased book one, *A Cry in the Moon's Light*, then you know this novella is a prequel to that story. If you haven't, you can learn what happens to Alessandra, Seth, and William in the exciting first book of this trilogy. I hope you enjoyed spending time in the Dark Forest with our heroine and are hungry for more.

I want to thank all those who left those humbling reviews. Reviews are priceless to authors such as myself, and I appreciate those who have taken the time to write them. If you like the story and haven't written a review yet, please take a moment to share your thoughts. The more reviews a book gets, the more publicity it receives. Let people know what you think and share the magic.

I also want to thank all the podcast listeners. The first podcast was named to Podbeans Top 10 Fiction Dramas of 2021, and this novella is also available in that audiodrama series.

Please consider supporting the podcast audiodrama by becoming a Patron Sponsor on Podbean. The production costs are high, and I could use all the help I can get to move forward with *The Undead Wars*.

For more information, you can follow me on Twitter or Instagram at @AlanMcGill14.

Sincerely,

Alan

ABOUT THE AUTHOR

Alan McGill is an American author who lives in northwestern Pennsylvania with a clowder of cats. Alan was close to his grandparents, who grew up during the Great Depression. They were married young and remained together until his grandmother's passing. His grandfather served in the Navy during WWII and was a gifted storyteller who wove humorous tales about tough events. Alan grew up listening to these stories of right and wrong and watching fictional heroes—such as the Lone Ranger, Adam West's Batman, and Captain America—stand up to bullies and protect those who could not protect themselves. This inspired him to always do what was right in his own life and shaped his love of storytelling.

BOOK ONE OF THE EXCITING TRILOGY!

In a time of castles, muskets, and werewolves, a beautiful woman travels across the treacherous Dark Forest to be by the side of her dying grandmother. With only a young carriage driver to protect her, she must use her wits and all of her courage to cross the wild country—and to evade the mysterious beast who stalks her. You will learn as she does that only love can defeat evil.

What follows is a tale full of horror, mystery, and romance: gruesome murders at a village hidden deep in the forest, a castle that holds dark secrets, and a black wolf leading a deadly pack. Nothing is as it seems, and this journey has only just begun. The beautiful lady in the carriage will learn that only love can defeat evil, but is it love or danger that cries out to her in the deceitful light of the moon?

BOOK TWO
IN THE SERIES,
COMING SOON!

Believing the werewolf threat extinguished, the former Duchess of Harcourt remained in Trevordeaux after the death of her grandmother. Colonel Voelker and his Hessians retired to the city of Hessen-Cassel, in what is now known as Germany. The Carriage Driver found a new path on the sea, and Lord Parlimae mourned his son. They all go about their lives, with the events of the Dark Forest now a mere memory.

But evil does not let you forget so easily. Wicked night creatures infiltrate cities, spread chaos, and search for witches. The Undead Army, led by the dreaded Witch King, is nearly ready to strike the final blow on humanity. There can be nothing to oppose him.

Now, Alessandra de Moreau, must decide if she can work with the man who killed the one she loved. Only together will they be able to stop this army. She will have to become something more and fight like never before—if they are to survive the Undead Wars.

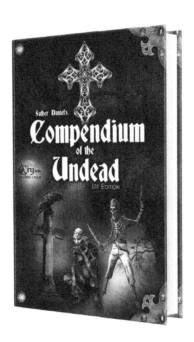

The must-have art and guidebook for the entire
world of A Cry in the Moon's Light!

This book has over seventy-five illustrations, character profiles,
scenes, places, maps, relics, and a full bestiary.

A CRY IN THE MOON'S LIGHT

PODCAST AUDIODRAMA

Includes the **Red Door** *Episodes*
A book you can hear!
*Sound FX * Music*
*and performances by Alan McGill, Linnea Sage,
Andrew Oakes, and Sarah Nightingale*

DARK FOREST

CAS

ABANDONED
CHURCH

MERCEL

Made in the USA
Monee, IL
23 May 2023

34095787R10096